ONE FOR SORROW

A Magpie Romantic Suspense Mystery

Marlow Kelly

Viceroy Press

ISBN: 978-1-9991430-3-9

Edited by Corinne Demaagd
From CMD Writing and Editing
https://cmdediting.com

Proofreading by
Gemma Brocato
https://www.gemmabrocato.com

CHAPTER ONE

The naked guy at the wheel of the stolen compact car made a sharp left turn, heading toward the bridge.

Officer Georgina Scott stomped on the gas. Her new partner, Liam Mackie, had a white-knuckled grip on the seatbelt strapped across his chest. She was pretty sure his right foot was pressed to the floor as he slammed on an imaginary brake.

"Officer Scott—Georgina—could you please—"

"Call me George. You don't have to worry. I've completed several advanced driving courses including pursuit, advanced emergency response, winter skills, and skid control," she explained as she cranked the steering wheel, following the suspect.

He stared straight ahead, ignoring her.

They'd received a call to apprehend a nude man who had stolen a red Mazda. He'd already crashed into a fence and sideswiped a truck.

This was not a normal occurrence in the town of Magpie, Alberta, but it wasn't the strangest thing that had ever happened either. Forty years ago, the town fathers had decided to develop the area into a holiday destination. They'd cleaned up the streets and lined them with Victorian fixtures, like lamp posts, and added floral arrangements, which gave the place an old-world appeal. Then they'd trucked in enough sand to make a beach on the shore of Charm Lake.

Magpie was just a two-hour drive west of Edmonton, and winter in Northern Alberta could last from October until April. That meant the town was packed with tourists in the warm summer months.

The long, hot days of June, when the sun didn't set until after eleven, meant more fun, but that fun sometimes led to inappropriate behavior, like stealing a car.

"Where does he think he's going? That way only leads to

the campground, a few private acreages, and the dump." Liam seemed to have found his voice.

The car thief slowed on the narrow bridge.

"Thank God." This was her chance. She gunned the engine, drawing alongside the rear of the vehicle. She waited until they had cleared the bridge deck and rammed her front bumper into the Mazda's side. The driver lost control, and the stolen car spun across the road and came to a stop in a ditch.

A young male jumped out and ran.

"Shit." Liam eyed the short man as though he were a four hundred-pound, machine gun-toting maniac. "Do you think he'll put up a fight?"

George put the SUV in park and scrambled out. "Yes, he will. We have to make sure he doesn't go in the river." She had no idea if the perpetrator could swim or not and didn't want to find out. At this point, the Charm River flowed out of Charm Lake at a slow, steady rate, but within a few miles, it drained into the North Saskatchewan River. The larger waterway was known for its depth and fast current, especially in the summer.

Naked Guy zigged as she zagged, avoiding her attempt to corral him. Finally, he pivoted on his heel and ran toward the town.

She raced after him. He skidded to a halt in the middle of the bridge deck and stared at an old-time lamp post, which was integrated into the guardrail.

She stopped dead six feet behind him, not winded by the short sprint. Liam came to a standstill on her left. He wasn't gasping or out of breath. Maybe he was as fit as he looked.

In her experience, people who had stripped out of their clothing and were behaving erratically were usually high on angel dust. Which meant they always fought like possessed demons. She could spot a PCP user in lockup because they were bare and wearing two pairs of handcuffs.

It was hard to gain any information about the suspect from looking at him. He was on the small side with a slight build and short, messy dark hair. He reached out a hand to swat at the lamp but missed because the light was too tall. He tumbled sideways and then straightened.

George crept closer to the suspect's right side, being careful not to make any sudden moves. Liam pointed to Naked Guy's left, signaling his intention to slip behind him.

A young lady with expensive blond highlights ran toward them. "I don't know what's wrong with him!"

Liam held up a hand. "Stay back."

"Is he a friend of yours?" George took in her pricey high heels and the pink designer purse slung over her shoulder.

The woman obeyed Liam's command and halted. "Yes. We're staying in the campground with friends."

"And you are?" Liam asked the question but kept his gaze on Naked Guy.

"Veronica." She swallowed hard as she clamped her arms across her chest. "Veronica Sitwell."

"What's his name?" George snapped on a pair of latex gloves and pointed to the perpetrator who reached for the lamp again—and missed again.

"Nicholas Gagnon." Veronica's lower lip quivered. "Everyone calls him Nick."

George kept Nick in her peripheral vision as she questioned Veronica. "Has Nick taken any drugs, is he on any medication, or does he have any conditions we should know about?"

"No, he had a few beers."

"Nothing else?" George made sure her demeanor was forceful and tough.

Veronica looked at her feet and then at Nick. "He also had a joint."

"Don't go anywhere. We'll need you to give a statement." George inched closer to Nick, who was now screaming disjointed words at the lamp.

"This is not a normal reaction to marijuana." Liam followed her lead, stuffing his hands into a pair of black latex gloves.

"No, but the nearest cannabis store is over an hour's drive away." Although marijuana was legal in Canada, it could only be legally purchased from a licensed supplier.

"You think he brought his product from a drug dealer?"

"Yes, there's a dealer in town who laces his weed with fentanyl, or PCP, to get users hooked on his products." *Damn it.* It had to be her father, Hank. To the general population, Hank Scott seemed like a charming man who owned a janitorial business, when in reality he was a man who traded in the misery and suffering of others, including his family.

When she'd joined the Magpie Police Service five years ago, she'd dreamed of seeing Hank behind bars, but it hadn't happened. No matter how close Chief Hunt got to an arrest, Hank was always one step ahead.

Two months ago, Chief Hunt had suffered a heart attack and had been forced to retire for health reasons. George knew her mentor's one regret was leaving the job without seeing Hank brought to justice.

Liam winced when Nick kicked the bridge wall. "Shit."

Nick didn't seem to notice the cuts on his feet. He must've trodden on something sharp because with every step he left a trail of blood.

Liam was new to the Magpie Police Service. This was their first shift together, and she hadn't had a chance to question him about his experience. He was tall, broad, and powerful. It would be easy for him to overpower a man as slight as Nick, but George saw the uncertainty in his gaze. It took practice to wrestle an individual who was unclothed. There was nothing to grasp except skin, and no one wanted to touch Nick's junk.

Liam nodded toward Nick, who grabbed the bridge wall. He looked like he might be preparing to hoist himself over. "We need to act soon before he goes into the water."

"Are you ready?" George checked that her security holster was fastened so Nick wouldn't be able to grab her Sig Sauer. She edged nearer, being sure not to use any sudden moves.

"Go," Liam shouted.

George lunged.

Nick screamed and scrambled onto the bridge wall.

She grabbed him by the waist and threw him onto the sidewalk. He landed face down. She pounced, pressing down on his back, and tried to grab his wriggling hands so she could cuff him. Nick shrieked again and tried to crawl away. George wrapped her legs around his knees, hoping to immobilize him. Nick tried to turn, but she used her weight to her advantage and held him in place.

With a roar, Nick pushed to all fours and then to a standing position. It was an amazing feat of strength. She clung to Nick's shoulders as he swung around. He roared again and then charged, heading for the bridge wall.

"Do something," George yelled. All she could do was hold on.

Liam charged and tackled them, slamming into Nick from the front. Momentum drove them sideways, away from the guardrail. George's arms were wrapped around Nick's neck as he toppled to the left. Everything slowed. She had no control. Her muscles went limp. Her elbow crashed into the pavement. Liam landed on top of them with Nick squashed in the middle. The impact drove the air from her lungs. Her head hit the sidewalk. Pain flashed through her skull, and then nothing.

****

"Officer down, officer down." Liam Mason sat on the yelping Nick as he shouted into the radio attached to his shoulder. He snagged one of Nick's arms as the druggie cried and tried to hoist himself up again, but Liam was too heavy to budge. He snapped on the handcuffs. Nick tugged at the restraints, trying to break free.

Two officers, whose names he couldn't remember, attached a second pair of cuffs to Nick's wrists and led the howling man away.

He rushed to Georgina's side just as the ambulance arrived. Blood oozed onto the pavement from a wound at the back of her head. He checked her breathing and was grateful to see the slight rise and fall of her chest.

Medics elbowed him out of the way. They were professional and efficient, checking her vitals and placing an oxygen mask over her face.

She was prettier than her photo with long dark hair, luminous green eyes, and the smoothest complexion he'd ever seen. Her lean, fit body looked good, even in her ugly-ass uniform. Not that her attractiveness mattered to his investigation.

According to her file, she was the daughter of a drug dealer, Hank Scott. Five years ago, she had managed to convince the former Magpie police chief, Aiden Hunt, to hire her. Now the new chief, Grayson Evans, had to deal with the fallout. A large number of drugs, mainly heroin, fentanyl, angel dust, and oxycodone had disappeared from the evidence locker of the Magpie Police Service, in what was believed to be a series of thefts. Most of it had ended up in the hands of her father. It didn't take a genius to figure out who had stolen them. Chief Evans had asked the Royal Canadian Mounted Police, known as the RCMP, to investigate because it was protocol. The RCMP were a national police force and members had jurisdiction as a peace officer in all parts of Canada. Liam Mackie, rookie Magpie Police constable was his undercover persona. Although, things weren't going exactly as he'd planned.

The medics placed Georgina on a stretcher and wheeled her into the ambulance.

Shit. He had knocked out his prime suspect on the first day working the case.

CHAPTER TWO

George scrubbed her face with her hands and groaned. The bright overhead bulb burned her eyes. She closed them and rubbed at her head, trying to loosen the bandage that had a vice-like grip on her skull.

But there wasn't one.

Using her fingertips, she massaged her scalp. Her hair was sticky, and her skin felt too tight, as if squeezing her brain. She found a swollen, tender wound on the left side that was held together with stitches. Someone had obviously tried to knock some sense into her. *Fat chance.*

She narrowed her eyes, just enough to allow a sliver of light. If she kept her eyelids half-closed and didn't move, she could look around without that sharp, stomach-churning pain. Her room, if you could call it that, was made up of three ugly multicolored curtains. The head of her bed rested against the only solid wall. A monitor by her side registered her steady heartbeat. A needle pierced the crease of her left elbow. Hopefully, it was just a saline drip. No strong medication for her. Just a couple of aspirin, and she'd be good to go. As soon as she could move without the all-encompassing headache, she would tear it out.

It was obvious she was at the Magpie Community Hospital, but couldn't seem to grasp the sequence of events that had landed her here. The last thing she remembered was meeting Liam at the station and shaking his hand. She tried to sit up and was hit with a wave of nausea. She let go of her questions as she lay back down. The hospital was a safe place. There was no need to worry.

She ran her hands along her body, no pants and no shirt, just a soft cotton gown.

A middle-aged nurse with dark hair, which was cut in a short bob, slipped through a gap in the curtains. "Good, you're awake."

Her neon scrubs made George squint. She closed her eyes to guard against the glare. "Yes." She was surprised by how dry and thready her voice sounded.

"The doctor will be in to see you soon." The nurse disappeared, not waiting for an answer.

The swish of the drapes accompanied with the thud of footsteps told her she had another visitor.

"Don't you know you're not supposed to sleep when you have a concussion?" The booming voice of Chief Evans ricocheted through her, making her moan. He was a bulky, bald man with saggy jowls, which suggested he was in his mid-fifties. It was rumored he'd worked for the Toronto Police Service for twenty years and had put away several organized crime bosses. The Magpie Police Service with less than twenty staff and only nine officers must seem small to him.

She forced herself to clamp her mouth shut, resisting the urge to tell him to go away. After taking a moment to bury her temper, she said, "You've got my gun and my personal effects?" It was important that her weapon was accounted for.

"Yeah, we got it. Don't worry about that. Do you remember what happened?" He pulled up a chair, scraping it along the floor.

She grunted and covered her face with her hands. "No."

"You were wrestling a naked man. He was slipped a dose of angel dust in a joint."

An image of the bridge across the Charm River formed in George's mind. "Do you think he knew he was taking PCP?"

"His friends don't think so. I see your Dad's hand in this." The chief wagged a fat finger at her as if it was her fault.

She winced. "Hank is not my dad. A dad is someone who takes you to a hockey game and makes sure you have food. A dad doesn't push you down the stairs for fun or kick you out of the house in a blizzard so he can do his drug deals in private."

"Blood is thicker than water."

"Wanna bet?" No matter how many times she explained, Chief Evans refused to believe she genuinely loathed Hank. "If it were up to me, he would already be in jail. I'm just a community cop. You're the chief. You have big city experience. Why haven't you called in the RCMP to investigate and build a case?"

He stood, refusing to acknowledge her demand for justice. "You'll probably be off work for a few days. Report in when you get back."

George breathed a sigh of relief once he was gone. She appreciated his forthright manner even though it was obvious he didn't like her. As long as they got along professionally, she could live with his curt responses that bordered on rudeness and the insinuations about her relationship with Hank.

She didn't do the job to score points with him. She did it for the people of Magpie. As a community police officer in small-town Alberta, it was her job to meet with people, ask for their input, visit schools, and help the disadvantaged. This wasn't like television. She didn't solve crimes; she solved problems, gave out tickets, and arrested those who caused a disturbance. She didn't investigate.

Now that she was injured, she wouldn't be able to train Liam, which meant she would be assigned another partner. The chief might put her with Greg Nicolson again. Greg was a decent, easy-going guy who didn't have a duplicitous bone in his body. Unfortunately, he was also out of shape. When they were out on patrol, it was up to her to pursue the suspects, which wasn't too bad. Alan Hammond, who was another officer she'd partnered with, was fit and chased suspects, but he tried to get out of doing paperwork. In her opinion, Alan's was the greater sin.

The only good thing about being knocked out was that Liam now had to complete the report on Nick. Huh, she remembered Naked Nick. It was a comfort to be able to recall the event that had landed her here. Not that she took any pleasure in Nick's situation, but not knowing was disturbing. She smiled and then winced as the slight upturn of her lips made it feel as though tiny drills were piercing her temples. She forced herself to relax her features.

Maybe partnering with Greg again would be a good thing. Liam's scent was distracting, which was odd because she'd never noticed a man's odor before. He didn't smell bad, just different.

Liam poked his head through the curtains. "Are you up for a visitor?"

She jolted upright, feeling like a child caught with a handful of stolen candy. Pain knifed through her skull and spiraled down her spine, followed by a wave of nausea.

He grabbed her shoulders, steadying her.

She inhaled a deep cleansing breath and exhaled, praying for some control. Throwing up in front of him would not be cool.

Her reaction showed just how fuzzy her thought processes were. Even though they'd only met an hour before they went on patrol, she shouldn't be surprised to see him. If he had been injured, instead of her, she would have visited.

"Sorry, I didn't mean to startle you." He urged her down but didn't release her when she was flat on her back. Instead, he stood over her, staring intently into her eyes. She tried to meet his gaze if only to prove she was fine, but she was too tired and out of sorts for a staring contest, especially with an appealing fellow officer.

He didn't have the good looks of a Hollywood actor. His dark hair was shaved so short she could almost see his scalp. His brown eyes were a little too far apart, and the tip of his nose bent down as though it had been crushed against something hard. But he had an inner quality that made him attractive. What it was, she couldn't say. It wasn't like her to get distracted by a man's scent or his magnetism. The knock to her skull must have caused some brain damage.

He nodded, as if he had answered some unasked question, and then let go of her shoulders and stood upright. "That was an interesting first day." He pushed a button, and a mechanical hum sounded as the electric motor raised the bed.

She didn't smile at his attempt at humor. "Just bad luck, I guess. How long was I out?"

"A couple of hours." He gazed at the wall behind her. "I'm sorry. I don't know my own strength."

She remembered the force with which Liam had tackled them

and then falling as she clung to the suspect's back. "As I said, just bad luck. If I'd landed on my shoulder instead…" She didn't finish because it didn't matter. They'd both done what needed doing, and going over the "what ifs" wasn't going to change anything. She shook her head, dismissing her own observation, and then moaned, once again, regretting the movement.

"Is there anyone I can call for you?" He poured her a glass of water and gently pressed it to her lips.

She took hold of the glass. While she appreciated his gesture, she wasn't an invalid and wouldn't allow him to treat her as one. The first sip didn't seem to reach her throat. It was absorbed by the dry tissues of her mouth. She took another sip and relished the feel of the cool liquid coating her dry, scratchy throat.

Finally, she answered his question, "My sister just left for two weeks' vacation in Hawaii with her boyfriend." She would've loved to see Grace, who was a smiling, cheerful soul. She always knew the right thing to say. Just being in her company made George happy. Grace had her act together. She was in a committed relationship and ran her own business. George couldn't imagine her life being that stable or successful.

"Your parents?" He sat in the visitor's chair, extending his long legs. His muscled thighs stretched the thick black fabric of his uniform pants, and the seams of his shirt strained at the shoulders, accentuating his shape.

"No." Her parents were divorced, thankfully. There was no way in hell she would ever call Hank, and her mother, Tina, suffered from an anxiety disorder. Once she started to worry, she spiraled downward. George didn't want her mom to suffer. She was better off not knowing. Besides, it was just a concussion. There was no need to fuss.

"The doc says you're going to be fine. She thinks you'll be back on your feet in no time. They'll keep you in overnight for observation." His words echoed her thoughts.

She changed the subject, not wanting to talk about her condition. "Are you okay?"

"Sure." His lips pressed into a grim line.

"And Naked Nick, was he hurt?"

He raised an eyebrow. "'Naked Nick'? That name's gonna stick." Then he shrugged. "He has some cuts. You were the only one seriously injured in the tussle, but he—"

"It's hard to tell until he comes down." George knew there would be a myriad of evaluations, tests, and assessments in Nick's future. For all they knew, he could've broken bones and wouldn't notice the pain until the drug wore off.

They fell into an uncomfortable silence. George had no idea what to say. She eyed him without turning her head. "Tell me about yourself. Are you married? Do you have a family?"

"No, and no to kids, too. My parents and sister live in Vancouver." He frowned and shook his head. It was a slight movement. If she hadn't been paying attention, she would've missed it.

"I've always wanted to visit Vancouver and drive the Sea to Sky Highway." She'd watched travel shows. It was a vibrant city on the pacific coast of British Columbia and was sandwiched between the sea and the mountains. "Do you get to see your family often?"

"Not really." He didn't smile or show any emotion when he talked about them. Maybe they weren't on good terms.

"Where did you work before Magpie?" She felt as though she were interrogating him.

"I worked for the RCMP for a couple of years and then here."

It was the bare bones of his story. She knew there had to be more. A couple normally meant two. She was twenty-six and guessed he was four or five years older than her, which meant he was probably around thirty. He could've become a cop at twenty-eight. That wasn't unheard of, but... She let it slide because her head pounded. It was as though a vein was throbbing inside her brain. Every heartbeat felt like a tiny explosion.

Then something occurred to her. "Hey, how come the doctor has told you about my condition and hasn't said one word to me? I'm the patient. He should be talking to me, not you."

"The doctor's a she." He smiled, the corner of his mouth curling up on one side. "She'll be in soon." As if on cue, the curtain was pushed aside and the small, slim frame of Doctor Sullivan stepped into the cubicle. George had talked to her on several occasions, normally concerning a victim, never about herself.

****

Liam stood outside Georgina's cubicle. The emergency room doctor, with a surprisingly unhurried manner, ordered him out while she talked to her patient.

"With all the leaps you've made in modern medicine, you'd think someone would have invented a hospital gown where your butt wasn't hanging out," Georgina grouched.

Liam tried not to picture her perfect butt. Respecting her need for privacy, he walked away. He didn't need to listen to the diagnosis. He'd been there. He knew what had happened. Besides, a cup of coffee might steady his nerves.

He wandered through the white-painted halls, hating the antiseptic smell that was endemic to all hospitals. He shouldn't have been so forceful when he tackled Georgina and the druggie. She had taken the full impact of the blow. Naked Nick had been crammed between them and therefore protected. He clenched his fists as he remembered the sickening thud as her head slammed into the curb.

It was close to midnight, and the cafeteria only had a selection of stale pastries and even staler coffee. He gratefully munched on a day-old Danish and added sugar to the brew to make it palatable. The first swallow burned like acid in his stomach. He pushed the cup aside.

Allowing himself to be swamped by guilt wasn't helpful. The loose-hanging hospital gown had revealed cigarette burns on her left forearm. The scarring looked old. If he had to guess, he'd say they were the work of her father. Maybe she was still being physically coerced into doing his bidding. If that were the case, he would help her. She would have to make a full confession and testify against him, but there was a good chance she wouldn't do any jail time.

None of his interactions with her explained his emotional

13

turmoil or why he was so off-balance. As a corporal with the RCMP, he'd worked money laundering and drug operations before. This assignment was part of an Alberta-wide taskforce to bring down a drug network. This was his third undercover mission. In the past, he'd always stuck to the same backstory. His name was Liam Mackie. He had no family and had grown up in foster care, but with her, he'd blurted out the truth, his truth. He really was from Vancouver, and his parents and sister did still live there. He had no idea why he'd let his guard down. Perhaps it wasn't about her. Maybe he was starting to burn out and was done with undercover work. The RCMP moved their members on a regular basis. The longest he'd been stationed in a detachment was six months. He was thirty years old and wanted a home, a place to call his own.

Maybe Georgina had thrown him off his game. There was something striking about her. When he'd grabbed her shoulders and studied her face, he'd hope to see signs of guilt or remorse. In his experience, most criminals had tells; small expressions that revealed their shame, such as not being able to meet his gaze, twitching, or shifting about. Many women touched a piece of jewelry or the base of their throat. His technique could be unnerving for the suspect, but it had paid off too many times for him to discount it.

But instead of studying her, he had been sucker-punched by her pale gray eyes. He could have sworn they were green when they'd met at the station.

She was pretty. That was just a fact, which he'd known after reading her file. She had a vulnerable quality, but she didn't come across as weak. Even from her hospital bed, with dried blood in her hair, he could sense her inner strength. Not surprising considering she was trained in jiu-jitsu, something that had been apparent when she'd tackled Naked Nick.

He took another sip of his coffee. He had to remember she wasn't your average suspect. She had been groomed from an early age to understand the organized business behind drug addiction. She'd probably grown up telling lies and hiding secrets.

The pretty face and great body masked a woman who had con-trived to get herself a position with the Magpie Police Service in order to get her hands on the drugs in the evidence locker and pass them to her father.

It was obvious she wouldn't be able to work for a few days, which put a crimp in his scheme to get close to her and figure out how she had accessed the secure area. But the plan was still the same. Her injuries just meant things would take a little longer than anticipated.

CHAPTER THREE

Liam watched as Georgina chatted with Lillian Field, the civilian office manager for the Magpie Police Service. It was Lillian who had reported the missing drugs to Chief Evans. She was a short, round woman in her mid-thirties, whose job involved a considerable amount of contact with police officers, court personnel, and the general public. By all accounts, she was the motherly type who brought cookies to work. Everyone he'd spoken to liked and trusted her.

He'd received his assignment for the evening. He was, of course, working with Georgina, and they were due on patrol at four. He just needed her to get her butt in the car.

"Let's have coffee next week." Lillian smiled as she scanned Georgina's paperwork and handed it to her.

Georgina hesitated, rubbed the back of her neck as though it was stiff, and then said, "I'm off Tuesday." She didn't seem the least bit worried about being late for her shift.

"I have a new muffin recipe. You'll love it." Lillian's job also involved cataloging and filing evidence. She appeared to genuinely like Georgina. Had the older woman let her guard down around a friend? That would explain how Georgina had gained access to the lockup.

Georgina laughed at something Lillian said and then turned to leave. Her smile disappeared when she saw him. Dark circles shadowed her eyes, even though she'd spent a day and a half at home recovering from her concussion. "Sorry, have you been waiting long?"

For a moment, he felt like a twelve-year-old watching a magic trick. Her eyes had changed color again and were now silver. He regained his composure and said, "Shall we go?"

"You drive." Georgina tossed him the keys as she pushed her way through the door. He caught the fob and clicked a button to unlock the vehicle as he followed her to the parking lot.

He squeezed into the driver's seat of the Ford SUV. Like all police cars, the interior was cramped. Every inch of space accommodated the equipment needed to do the job. The center console housed radio equipment, a laptop, light switches, siren switches, and a portable radio charger.

Georgina climbed in the passenger seat. She didn't seem to notice the lack of room, but as a patrol cop, she was probably used to it. "I assume you've been out with other officers since Friday. I'll show you the way I do things, then you can take everything you've learned and decide what works for you."

"Sounds good."

"Lakeshore Drive runs parallel to Main Street. I start at the Credit and Savings Bank near the river and follow Lakeshore Drive until I reach the sports center at the far end. Then I turn onto Main Street and head back towards the bank and the river. That way I check the beach for problems first. It's early, and Sunday evenings are usually quiet, but you never know."

"Got it." He pushed the ignition button, and the SUV purred to life. He'd studied a map of Magpie before his first shift and was familiar with the geography of the town. It was small with just two main roads which, not surprisingly, ran parallel to the lake. They had a decent sports center that doubled as a community center. The town also boasted a bar, a coffee shop, two restaurants, a grocery store, a gas station, and a marine repair shop. None of it screamed drugs and corruption.

He hadn't been on shift since her concussion two days ago. Chief Evans was in charge of his schedule, but maybe he should have gone out with the other officers and watched them work. That way he would be able to compare Georgina's conduct with theirs. It was also unfortunate that her injury had robbed him of the chance to watch her process Naked Nick.

She placed her right elbow against the passenger door and propped her head up with her hand. "I work my way through downtown and out to the residential area on the other side of the highway. Greg Nicholson and Alan Hammond are patrolling

17

the campground and the outlying areas, including the rest of the lake's shore, but they'll provide backup if we have any trouble with tourists."

She seemed tired. He thought about asking her if her head hurt but decided against it. He wasn't here to become her friend.

"Sounds good." He put the SUV in drive. "There's no room for advancement in the Magpie Police Service. Have you thought about transferring to the RCMP?" If she'd tried for a promotion and failed, that might be a motive for the thefts. But then again, the cigarette burns on her arm might be all the reason she needed.

"No."

"What? Never?" By all accounts, she was a good officer, that is if he ignored the fact she was a crooked cop.

"No, I'm not interested in climbing the ladder."

That was an interesting statement, but she was probably of more use to her dad working as a beat cop. That way she would have access to narcotics. "You want to wrestle drunks and druggies for the rest of your life?"

"No, of course not." She rubbed her forehead, seeming fatigued. "I just don't see myself spending the rest of my life in Magpie."

He wasn't sure what to make of her statement. "Why not? It seems like a nice town."

She pointed to a well-kept, cedar storefront with a wooden deck that provided outdoor seating. "Do you see that coffee shop over there?"

"The Jumping Bean?" It was half café, half gift shop. Liam had made stopping there part of his morning routine. Sitting outside sipping coffee while he soaked in the view of the picturesque lake and watched the townspeople go about their business was an invigorating way to start the day.

"It's owned by Mrs. King, the mayor's wife. She is a judgmental, stuck-up woman who, when she sees me, always makes a face as if she smelled something bad. I'm tired of being judged. One day I'll move away and start fresh where no one knows me."

"I take it she's not your favorite person," he said, adding a sarcastic edge to his tone.

She stared out the passenger window. "No, she's not."

He couldn't see her expression, but he had a feeling there was more to the story. "How do you know she's a judgmental, stuck-up person?

"Experience. This town is a mix of small business owners who rely on tourism, oilfield workers, and farmers. They're mostly an honest, hardworking bunch." She ignored his question.

"And homeless people." He pointed to an old man with a long white beard who was climbing out of a dumpster located next to the Chinese restaurant.

"That's Smokey. He's not homeless. You know how Lakeshore Drive turns into a dirt trail by the sports center?"

He nodded.

"Smokey lives in an old cabin on that section of road. Stop the car. I'll introduce you."

He did as he was told, pulling into an angled street spot.

She opened her door but didn't get out. "He used to be a money man in Calgary, but he had a breakdown and followed his daughter here. She was working at the Charm Hotel for the summer. She left to go back to university, and he stayed." She then stepped out of the vehicle and waved at the old man.

Liam followed her to the sidewalk. "When you say 'money man,' I assume you mean he was into stocks and bonds."

She nodded.

"How does he earn a living now?" He didn't care about the answer, but it seemed like a normal thing to ask.

"He's on disability, and he collects things to supplement his income."

"Collects things?"

"Junk." She was familiarizing him with the locals to better prepare him for the job. "He goes to the dump and searches for anything he can find of value, then he sells it. I like to refinish furniture in my spare time. So occasionally he'll tell me about a piece that looks promising. He helps me haul it home where I can work on it. Then I get him to sell it."

This was news. There had been no hobbies listed in her file. In fact, it contained very little personal information. Just the basics, which included a report on her family and the fact that she was single. Her interests might not matter, but they were a window into her psyche. He also wondered how much money she made from her side business and whether she declared it on her tax return. It would probably be petty to charge her with such a crime. Generally, Canada wasn't as strict as the USA in enforcing jail time for tax evasion, but it could happen. And if it was good enough for Al Capone, it was good enough for a small-town Alberta cop.

"Smokey," she called as they approached.

The man with long white hair and a beard to match popped out from behind the dumpster. He wore a filthy white dress shirt with an equally dirty tie. "If it isn't Georgie Girl. I heard you banged your head."

"It's all better now. I'd like to introduce you to Officer Mackie. He's the latest recruit to the Magpie Police Service."

The old man stared at Liam and then raised one eyebrow. "He looks too young and ambitious to be one of ours."

Liam said nothing to Smokey's astute observation.

"Be nice," Georgina warned. "I haven't been to the dump in a while. Have you seen any good pieces?"

"Let me get this straight. You collect old furniture and fix it up?" Liam crinkled his nose at the idea of handling anything that had been found in the garbage.

She gave him a small smile and then flinched as if the action pained her. "I only work with wood furniture. Nothing uphol-stered. And I check for woodworm or any kind of infestation. You'd be surprised at how much solid wood gets thrown out be-cause it's scratched. It only takes a little work to strip it down and sand out the scuffs and varnish it."

Smokey jumped to her defense. "She makes it look like new and never takes a penny for herself. Donates it all to the homeless. People love her work. She could be a professional."

"I guess one man's trash really is another man's treasure." He would have to look into this side business of hers and check to see if she really gave all her income to charity. It all sounded a little too good to be true.

Georgina waved at the old man. "See you around."

Smokey gave them an absent wave as he studied the contents of the bin.

Liam squeezed back into the SUV. "Where to now?"

"Turn left at the end of the block by the pub."

He eyed the Rockin Horse Saloon as they drove past. Faded cladding covered the exterior. Paint peeled from the door and window frames, making the place appear neglected.

"Have you met Mattie Rogers?" Using her fingertips, she massaged her temples.

He shook his head.

"She owns the Rockin Horse. She may look tough, and her place might not be refined, but she has a heart of gold."

"Do you get a lot of trouble with drunk tourists?" It was the kind of question a new officer would ask.

Georgina closed her eyes for a second too long, but then opened them and blew out a breath. "Sometimes, like the other night. The beach has always been popular. In the last couple of years, the town has expanded its amenities to include better hotels, ATV and biking trails, fishing, and hiking. That means more tourists and more partying.

"Chief Evans thinks your dad is responsible for Naked Nick."

She clenched her jaw as she rubbed her left forearm. "Please don't call Hank Scott my dad. He was the sperm donor. Nothing more."

"Wow. Do you really have no feelings for the guy?" Liam had his own issues with his family, but he found it hard to believe she could disown her father completely.

****

George put her hand to her head, wishing it didn't still ache.

The doctor had given her a prescription for codeine, but she refused to take anything stronger than aspirin. "Listen, I wanted to be the first to tell you, but I guess the moment's gone."

"Tell me what?" Liam kept his gaze on the road. He steered their police car past the family restaurant and then turned right, heading away from downtown Magpie.

Fatigue overwhelmed her, which was strange because she'd slept for the last two days. Maybe she needed more coffee. "Hank Scott is the mastermind behind the drug trade in Magpie."

"You're kidding." He raised an eyebrow, his expression a little too exaggerated to be genuine.

"Are you trying to pretend you don't already know? You just said Chief Evans thinks Hank is responsible for what happened to Naked Nick."

He gave her a sideways glance accompanied by a sheepish grin. "Not working, huh?"

"No, it's not." She might as well explain everything. "Hank is a clever man who understands that the most successful businesses are ones with repeat customers. It's kind of like a good hair stylist. Your hair keeps growing, you need it cut, and you'll keep going back to someone who does a good job. Hank's always working toward that repeat customer. He's also smart enough not to attract unwanted attention by being violent."

Explaining her past never got any easier. "What else have you heard?" She might as well get the inevitable innuendos and insulting hints over with. It wouldn't be anything she hadn't heard before.

His brows creased as he thought about his answer. "You convinced Chief Hunt to give you a job, but there are those who think you pulled the wool over an old man's eyes."

"That idea is utterly ridiculous. Aiden Hunt was the sharpest cop I've ever known. No one got anything past him, and those who think I tricked him either weren't with the department or have conveniently forgotten how Hank tortured me, my sister, and my mother."

They'd circled the town and had made their way past the gas

station. She pointed to their left. "Turn here. There's a hotel on the highway with a café. I need another coffee." She flinched as the sun reflected off a window, blinding her, making her head hurt even more.

Liam did as he was told, steering the SUV to a parking spot. Once he'd shifted into park, he swiveled in his seat, giving her his full attention. "When you say torture...?"

"He's a psychopath, and like all psychos, he's good at hiding his true nature."

His dark eyes snagged hers. She was caught in his gaze, staring at him for way too long. She should look away or say something to break the tension. Why was he staring at her? Finally, she turned, concentrating on an old-fashioned lamppost as if it were the most interesting thing in the world.

"You're saying he kills—"

"No. I said he was smart enough not to be violent. What did you study in college?" Looking around, she had the strangest feeling, as though she were seeing the area for the first time, which was nuts.

"Law." His hands gripped the steering wheel as though the answer troubled him.

"That figures. A law degree is a good way to go for a career cop. I took sociology with a few courses in psychology."

"There's a difference?" He grinned. The dimple on the left side of his face made him seem boyish and charming.

"Yes, my point is, most psychos aren't like Ted Bundy. They don't kill, but they have no conscience and are incapable of feeling guilt, shame, or remorse. Which means you have a person who will stop at nothing to achieve his goals."

"You sound like you did your research. And what are Hank's goals?"

"Money and power. Before I became a cop, I told Chief Hunt everything I knew about Hank's business. His contacts, his middlemen, where he gets his supply and how he gets his clients. Dealing drugs is a business, just like any other. Except it destroys lives." Someone was burning toast. She gazed up at the windows, expecting to see smoke billowing out.

They made their way through the lobby and joined the lineup in the busy café. Two young women worked the counter; one took the orders while the other prepared the drinks. She scanned the customers as she waited her turn. A light flashed in her eyes, blinding her again. She shook her head, which caused a stabbing pain to erupt at the base of her skull.

A handsome man with dark hair, graying at the temples, stood and then turned to face her. *Hank.* He wore his usual uniform of expensive jeans with an equally expensive short-sleeved, collared golf shirt. He would've traded his casual clothes for a suit if he lived in the city. Anything to fit in and appear normal.

He caught her with his hate-filled gaze and then smiled and patted his arm. It was a warning. One day he would hurt her again. It was only a matter of time. She stood tall and met his stare. She curled her hand into a fist, issuing her own silent threat. She would hurt him back. Without saying a word, he turned and walked away.

Her knees felt like rubber as she watched him retreat. She wanted to sit down, but she would be damned if she would show any weakness because of Hank Scott. Just the sight of him reminded her of who she used to be—a young, frightened girl.

"What was all that about?" Liam's question pulled her back to the present.

"That was Hank. He was sending me a signal."

"What was he saying?"

She tried to pull up her sleeve and explain Hank's intent, but her muscles were stiff. She opened her mouth, but the words came out garbled and distorted. Then everything dimmed.

She opened her eyes, surprised to find she was lying flat on her back. Liam peered down at her. She must've fainted. There was a disconnect between her and the rest of the world as though she were watching and hearing it, but couldn't participate.

Once again, she tried to speak, but couldn't form a coherent sound. She leaned on one elbow. Liam grabbed her shoulders and forced her down. She wanted to get up. It was embarrassing enough to have fainted in public. She slapped at his hands.

"Stay there." He had the pale, pinched look of someone in shock. He spoke into his radio, but she couldn't understand what he said.

He'd spoken in English. She knew that much, but the sounds were jumbled, their meaning unclear. Maybe he was right about her staying put. Perhaps if she lay here long enough, the world might make sense again. Besides, she was so exhausted, just the idea of moving seemed overwhelmingly strenuous. She closed her eyes and allowed her mind to drift.

CHAPTER FOUR

This time she'd been awake for the whole humiliating ordeal, the paramedics, the ride in the ambulance, being admitted to the hospital, and lying in the same cubicle she'd vacated just a few days ago. Liam said she'd had a seizure, but he had to be wrong.

She hated to admit it, but seeing Hank *had* gotten to her. His silent threat had reawakened all her anger and rage.

Magpie had a population of around two thousand. She not only saw her father all the time; she also couldn't get away from her reputation as the drug dealer's daughter.

She buried her memories. She could go over her childhood again, and again, but it wouldn't change a thing. She'd made the conscious choice to ignore her past and other people's opinions of her. She'd become a force for good. Once the doctor arrived, she would get a clean bill of health and go back to work protecting the community.

Doctor Sullivan pushed the curtain aside. As always, her petite figure was dwarfed by her white lab coat, which was buttoned from her neck to her knees. Today, her graying blond hair was braided.

She wrapped a blood pressure cuff around George's arm and pumped the bulb. "You're becoming a regular."

George faked a smile. She didn't want to be a regular.

"Your blood pressure's good. I need to ask you a few questions about how you felt just before the episode." She put the instrument away.

George rolled her eyes. "I just fainted. It wasn't an 'episode.'"

"Call it what you like. I still need you to answer some questions."

George nodded. "Let's get this over with."

"Before the epi— Before you passed out, did you have any feelings of anxiety, racing thoughts, déjà vu?" Doctor Sullivan read from a clipboard.

George shook her head.

"Or maybe the opposite, something felt unfamiliar even though it wasn't?" The doctor looked George in the eye.

She sucked in a breath. She had thought the parking lot seemed new and different somehow. She crossed and then uncrossed her arms, trying to make sense of everything. "I smelled burnt toast. That's a symptom of a stroke or something, isn't it?"

Doctor Sullivan gentled her tone. "It was probably a seizure. We need to establish if this was an isolated incident caused by your head injury or if you have epilepsy. You'll need to go for an Electroencephalogram, an EEG. That will tell us if you have..."

George stopped listening, her mind stuck on the word *epilepsy*, and what it would mean to her life and her work.

Doctor Sullivan carried on talking, seeming to need to get all the bad news out before her courage failed. "Although I'm not required by law to contact Alberta Transportation, you are. Your driver's license will be suspended until you've been seizure free for six months. At which time, you'll need a letter from a neurologist stating you're cleared to drive."

"What about my job?" Her need to help others gave her life meaning. Hank hurt people. She helped them. That was the way it was. The way it had to be.

"I don't know." Doctor Sullivan shrugged. "It'll take a few weeks to arrange the tests and an appointment with the neurologist. In the meantime, go home and get some rest." She disappeared through a gap in the curtains like a magician who had done the worst trick in history and didn't want to face her audience.

****

Liam sat in the emergency waiting room. A heavy, sick feeling cramped his stomach. The sight of Georgina having a seizure was the most disturbing thing he had ever witnessed. Every muscle in her body had gone rigid, and then she'd dropped like a fallen tree. It had all been so quick. She'd turned blue and stopped breathing as her unseeing eyes stared blankly into space. After thirty seconds, she'd come around, but she'd had a hard time talking.

One of the paramedics, who had escorted her to the hospital two days ago, told him that seizures were common after a head injury. *Shit.*

He had no idea if the damage to her brain was permanent or not. Establishing the extent of her injury would require tests, a lot of tests. She was banned from driving for at least six months, which meant she would be placed on sick leave until this mess could be sorted out.

Chief Evans ran into the waiting room as if he were late. "Is it true?"

"Is what true?"

"George had a seizure?"

"Yeah, probably brought on by her concussion." The imaginary lead weight in his stomach grew heavier. He was investigating her, which meant she would have to face the consequences of her actions. But right now, she was sick and injured because he had been too rough and knocked her out.

The chief fist-pumped the air. "Now I can fire her ass."

"Really?" Liam hated the role he'd played in this.

"Sure. She can't work so she's done." Chief Evans ran a finger across his throat and then stared at Liam as though the answer was obvious.

"I wouldn't do that if I were you." Liam grabbed his elbow and dragged him into a deserted hallway, ensuring they were alone. He didn't want any details of the investigation to leak out.

"Why not? Once she's gone, the supply to her father will be closed," Evans growled through clenched teeth.

"I think Hank Scott is threatening her."

"How?" Evans' jaw slackened as he visibly relaxed.

He pictured Hank in the coffee shop. "She has cigarette burns on her left arm. From what I can gather, Scott gave them to her. They look old. Just before her seizure, she had a non-verbal confrontation with her father. They stared at each other, he rubbed his arm, and then walked out."

"What does this mean for your case?" Chief Evans collapsed onto a black plastic chair. His toe tapped against the floor as though he'd had too much caffeine.

"I'm not sure yet. It could be a piece of the puzzle or it could be nothing." Hank Scott was definitely an abusive father. Georgina had stated that he was a psychopath. What had it been like growing up with a man like that?

"How far along are you?" Evans patted his knee, beating out a rhythm.

"Someone searched the police computer system for opioids, and then they accessed the evidence locker, opened the relevant packages, and took the pills. Whoever it was is good enough with computers to hide their identity." He took a seat opposite the chief.

"You're saying she looked through the files to see which cases involved hard core drugs so she knew where to look?"

"We can't be certain it was Georgina. On each occasion, she was on shift. It's circumstantial, and there are still some unanswered questions."

"Like what?" It must've been a shock for the new chief of police to discover the missing evidence. If it hadn't been for the efficient office manager, they probably still wouldn't have noticed the drugs had been stolen.

"She's not authorized to access the locker, so how did she get in?"

The chief shrugged. "Where there's a will..."

"You know that's not enough." Liam needed more than conjecture to convince him that Georgina was a thief and press charges. He wanted proof or a confession.

"So why can't I fire her?"

"Because she has rights. We haven't proven she's supplying her father. You called the RCMP because you wanted us to build a solid case. I'm going to do my best to give you that. But you can't do anything to make her suspicious." Liam stood and paced the small space, feeling restless and edgy. The chief's hatred for

Georgina was clouding his judgement, something that had the potential to damage the investigation.

Chief Evans rubbed his chin, thinking. "What do you suggest?

"I assume she's entitled to twenty-six weeks paid sick leave?"

The chief nodded.

"She'll need tests to find out what's wrong with her. That'll buy us some time and prevent her from accessing the drugs. I have to verify she's the one who read the files and not another member of your detachment. Then I have to prove she stole them. Let's work the case with an open mind and go where the evidence leads." He needed to refocus his efforts and put aside his guilt over her condition.

"What do you need me to do?"

"Treat her as you would any other cop who's been injured on the job. They gave her an x-ray, which was inconclusive. She will need more tests. In the meantime, I'll become her new best friend." In his experience, no one could tell plausible lies all the time. His best move was to befriend her and gain her trust. If he spent enough time with her, sooner or later she would reveal her true self.

CHAPTER FIVE

Liam slid into a booth facing the entrance of the Rockin Horse Saloon. The pub interior was just a large room decorated with varnished wood paneling. There was a long bar at one end, and booths lined the other three walls. A dance floor was in the center.

A woman stood at the cash register arguing with a younger man. She had curly salt-and-pepper hair, and he guessed her to be in her late fifties. Her pointed features, the lines around her mouth, and her cold, dark eyes gave her the look of a woman who'd had a hard life. Despite that, she was still attractive. Liam assumed she was the famous Mattie Rogers, the woman who had helped Georgina when she was a teen.

From his position, he could only see the back of the man's head. He had short brown hair, which suggested he was younger than Mattie.

Mattie thrust something into his hands and shoved him toward the exit, which was to the right of the bar.

The young man allowed the door to slam against the wall as he elbowed Greg Nicholson out of the way.

"Hey, watch it," Greg called.

He shook off his irritation, spotted Liam, waved, and then joined Liam in the booth. His once broad, muscled footballer's physique had turned to flab. His short brown hair showed no signs of graying, which combined with his easy-going disposition made him seem younger than his forty years.

"It's quiet in here tonight." Liam decided to keep the conversation light. The only thing he had in common with Greg was the job, which meant sooner or later they would get around to talking about Georgina.

Greg swiveled in his seat, waved at Mattie, and then said, "It's only seven. This place will be full by nine."

Mattie arrived balancing a pitcher of beer and two beer mugs on a tray. "I know Greg wants a jug and a glass. How about you?"

"I'm Liam." He smiled and gave her a small wave. "A glass is good." If he'd been drinking for pleasure, he'd have preferred a rye and ginger ale, but this was business disguised as pleasure, so he settled on a beer.

"Have you heard about George?" Greg asked Mattie.

She cocked her head to one side. "No, what about her?"

Greg's shoulders drooped. "She had a seizure. She's benched."

Mattie gasped. "That's awful. When did this happen?"

"Yesterday evening. I was with her," Liam added, once again burying his guilt. "The doctor thinks it was caused by the concussion she got a couple of days ago."

"I heard about the naked guy. What's going to happen to her now?" Mattie placed their drinks in front of them.

Greg looked at Liam and shrugged. "I guess she's on medical leave while they do tests but, as of now, she can't drive."

Mattie shoved her hand into the pocket of her apron. "That's terrible. I'll give her a call tomorrow and see if she needs anything."

"Maybe you should take her some of your awesome vegetables." Greg grinned at Liam. "Mattie grows the best tomatoes and potatoes you'll ever taste."

"That girl's not getting any of my veggies. You know as well as I do that health food is wasted on her. She doesn't appreciate my juicing."

"But she does make good coffee. Did you teach her that?" Greg smiled.

"Nope. She picked it up in college. I guess if something's important enough, you'll learn how to do it right." Mattie headed back to the bar.

"The chief was telling me that Georgina is connected to the drug trade in town." Liam hadn't planned on pushing, but they were already talking about her so he might as well make the most of the opportunity.

"You mean Hank Scott? That bastard is nothing but trouble."

Greg curled his upper lip, his disgust obvious.

"What are you saying? Like father, like daughter?"

Greg took a long gulp of his drink and then said, "Maybe and maybe not. George is intense and vengeful like her dad, but that's where the similarity ends."

"How do you mean?" Liam sipped his drink, resisting the urge to gulp it down. He wanted to keep a clear head.

"She's like the preacher's son who turns to crime, except the opposite." Greg took another long swallow.

"She's the criminal's daughter who became a cop." That was a different take.

"Exactly. Did you know she's the school liaison officer, and part of her job includes lecturing high school kids on the dangers of drug use?"

"Really?" Why hadn't Evans included that in her file?

"Oh, yeah. She's good, too. She tells them how the drug business works. How Hank Scott imports the stuff, divides and cuts the haul. Even if they don't buy drugs that contain formaldehyde, PCP, or heroine, they could still end up with something that contains glass or perfume. Then he recruits high school kids to sell to other kids at a low price because he knows once he has a customer, they will give him all of their money for the rest of their lives."

"Do they understand it all?"

"She makes sure they do. She dumbs it down for the lower grades. She has some really scary stories for the older kids. She makes a difference." Greg drained his glass.

"I wonder if she's ever tempted to take over his enterprise..." If she understood how the trade worked and had access to her father's connections, she could go into business for herself.

Greg shook his head. "I don't see it. She once put her dad in the hospital. She beat him up that bad."

"She what?" This was another piece of background that hadn't been included in the report. If this were true, it called into question everything he knew about her relationship with her father. "Were charges laid?"

"I guess not, or she wouldn't have been able to become a cop."

There was something off in Greg's answer. "Were you living in Magpie at the time?"

"No." He shook his head. "Word is, one of his suppliers wanted to bed Grace, George's little sister. She was only fourteen."

"Geez. Scott really is a sick bastard." He never got used to hearing about the awful things people did to their children.

"He sure is, and he doesn't give a shit about anything except himself. Anyway, somehow George got wind of it. She must've snapped. She beat the crap out of him. He ended up in hospital, and while he was gone, the mom and sisters got away."

"And then she came back to work here?" He couldn't imagine many victims of abuse returning to the place where their abuser had so much power.

"That was Chief Hunt's doing. I don't know how he managed to persuade her." Once again, Greg's words put a different slant on Chief Evans file. She hadn't persuaded an old man to give her a job. He had convinced *her*.

"I wonder how she feels now that Hunt's gone." The answer probably wasn't pertinent to his case, but his curiosity had been peeked.

"Vulnerable, I imagine. Evans isn't happy about having her on the team."

That was an understatement, but Liam decided to play dumb. "Really?"

"If you ask me, he treats her like his own personal punching bag." There was something in Greg's expression. His narrowed eyes and tight jaw telegraphed his distaste for the new police chief.

"You don't like him," Liam said, stating the obvious.

Greg sighed, pulled out his wallet, and threw some money on the table. "Maybe I'm old fashioned. If you have to chew someone out, do it in the privacy of your office and make sure it's for a legitimate reason. The day before you arrived, he was screaming at George because there was no coffee. Now, I'll admit she makes the best coffee I ever tasted, but it was the start of her shift, and it's not her job to keep him supplied with caffeine. She's an officer and deserves to be treated with respect." Greg's displeasure with his new boss was evident. And Liam had to admit he wasn't impressed with Evans' behavior so far. He would contact his superior, Sergeant Olsen, and have her do a background check.

Liam stood. "So is your wife waiting for you?"

Greg joined him and they strolled to the parking lot together. "Yeah, we're going to eat outside, have some wine, and watch the sun go down." Greg's round face lit up. "Unless the mosquitos swarm us. Then we'll take it inside and watch some TV."

Liam said goodbye to Greg and walked along Main Street. He turned at River Road, heading toward his apartment near the highway. He hadn't driven to the pub. It was a nice night, and he only lived a fifteen-minute walk away.

If it were true that Georgina had put her father in the hospital, it changed everything he knew about her. It would've taken a lot of anger for a seventeen-year-old girl to put a grown man, who was undoubtably stronger than her, in the hospital.

Georgina might not feel like a victim, and her personality profile would be completely different. So far, nothing about her was as cut and dried as it seemed.

CHAPTER SIX

George had vacuumed, dusted, cleaned her floors, and scrubbed her bathroom. All before nine o'clock in the morning. She considered working on the solid maple three-drawer dresser she was refinishing but decided against it. Sanding and staining the wood required focus, composure, and a steady hand. At this moment, she possessed none of these qualities.

She'd been released from the hospital after a couple of hours, but was under orders to return if she had another seizure. Her condition wasn't considered life-threatening, and the small community hospital needed the beds for more urgent patients.

She'd already received an email from the police union confirming she had been placed on sick leave. She would be paid a hundred percent of her salary. There were clauses about her situation changing, but she'd skipped over those.

Being banned from driving had turned her whole world upside-down. That was why she wanted to stay busy. That way she wouldn't have to think about not working and not knowing what shape her future would take.

She stepped out onto her small five-by-five deck. Her home wasn't fancy, but the location was fantastic. She rented a trailer on a private, treed, lakefront lot from a couple who lived in Edmonton. The property had belonged to an elderly relative who had since died. The sound of water lapping against the shore combined with the mature trees created a restful oasis. A place where she could unwind from the chaos of work.

This far away from town, the shoreline wasn't a groomed beach but a marsh with reeds, grasses, and trees at the water's edge. In the mornings before work, she sat on her porch, sipped her coffee, and watched the coming and goings of water birds, rabbits, and other small animals that lived in the wetland habitat.

She paced around her secondhand coffee table, which she'd refinished by staining the top in a dark cherry and giving the legs a white antique finish. The house was on the small side with only a living room, one bedroom, a bathroom, and a kitchen, but the windows were huge, which made the space seem light and airy. In the summer when the long hot days made it difficult to sleep, she would open them and drift off listening to the frogs singing.

Normally, she didn't mind the lack of space, but today she felt suffocated, as if the walls were closing in. She'd been on sick leave for less than a day and already had cabin fever. This didn't bode well for her ability to stay sane during her convalescence.

She brushed her teeth and then attacked her hair. Grace, a talented stylist who owned a chain of salons in Edmonton, had cut George's long dark mane into layers so it fell in place without any need for extra styling. She was wearing leggings and a tank top over a sports bra which, as far as she was concerned, was presentable. Unfortunately, some of the more old-fashioned citizens of Magpie would disagree with her. She shrugged into a white, long-sleeved shirt that came down to her thighs, stuffed her wallet and cell phone into her backpack that doubled as a purse, and grabbed her keys. She reached for the door and stopped.

What was she thinking? She couldn't drive her car. She was in good shape and worked out five days a week, which meant it would only take her twenty minutes to walk to downtown, but she still needed supplies. It was cool outside now, but it would be hot by noon. At this time of year, the mosquitos were out in full force. She grabbed her bug-spray and sunscreen from where she'd left them on the shelf next to the back door. Then she filled a reusable water bottle. She threw all the items into her bag. If she needed anything else, she'd have to buy it. She'd stroll around the shops, grab a cup of coffee, buy some groceries, and then walk back. That would fill most of her day and get her out of the house.

She peered out of the living room window at the sound of a

car on her gravel driveway. Lillian Field, the office manager for the Magpie Police Department, parked her new Chevrolet Tahoe behind George's ten-year-old Subaru. Lillian was so short George was surprised she could see over the steering wheel of her vehicle. She jumped down from the driver's seat and then walked to the passenger side to retrieve a plate covered in clear plastic wrap.

From her spot at the front door, George couldn't see what she was carrying but, knowing Lillian, it was something baked. She was the kind of woman who talked too much and was a little too friendly. Lillian laughed at George's jokes and seemed caring. But George always got the unshakable sense that something was off. She hadn't grown up in a caring environment. Perhaps, she was simply unnerved by Lillian's lack of reserve. Or maybe it was because, as a child, she'd watched Hank be charming and caring toward individuals, not because he liked them, but because he wanted something. There was no hiding from the fact that her childhood had damaged her to the point she was wary of Lillian's act of kindness.

George's only close female friend was her sister, Grace. Maybe she should look at making an effort with her personal relationships now that she had time to spare. But she couldn't, not today. She felt as if someone had taken a cheese grater to her existence, and she needed time to piece it back together.

Lillian gave George a big smile and held up the plate. "I brought cookies."

George tried to smile back but wasn't sure if she managed it.

"Nothing makes the world seem brighter than sugar." The older woman stuffed the baked goods into George's hand.

"I was just about to go out," George said, hoping Lillian would take the hint and leave.

"I won't stay long." She barged in, not taking off her shoes. From watching American TV, George had surmised that removing shoes when entering a home was mostly a Canadian custom, and as far as she knew, Lillian had lived in Alberta all her life, so she should know to remove her damn shoes instead of tracking dirt into George's home.

The older woman scrutinized the tiny room. "This is a nice place. You've done a good job decorating."

George ignored Lillian's discourteousness and gave the place a critical once-over. The floor was a cheap laminate, which was pale and matched the white walls. It wasn't great, but it was clean. "All the credit goes to my landlord."

Lillian rubbed her hands together. "I'm so sorry about what's happened."

George didn't say anything. She was sorry, too, but stewing over it wasn't going to make it go away.

"How long do you think you'll be off work?"

George shrugged as she held the door open, basically telling Lillian, without words, to leave. "I'll know more after the tests."

"And when will that be?" Once again, Lillian focused on the house.

"I'm waiting to hear." George had invited Lillian over for coffee several times. Not because she was particularly comfortable with her, but because the older woman had shown an interest in George's life. It had never happened, and maybe that was for the best. From the way Lillian eyed her eclectic furnishings, George had a feeling she was being judged and had been found wanting.

Finally, Lillian turned to face her. Her normally cheerful face was scrunched into a ball as though she'd tasted something sour. "It's all very vague."

George sighed. *Vague.* Yes, that was her life at the moment. She had no idea what the future would hold. When she'd woken on Friday, she'd had a path, a direction. Now, on Monday, she was adrift. No, not yet. If her seizure was an isolated incident, she could go back to her life and put all this behind her. "I have no control over it. I'm trying to go with the flow."

"Well, I shouldn't keep you." Lillian made a beeline for the front door. "I have to make sure everything's ready for the audit."

"Good luck." An independent audit had been ordered by Chief Evans when he'd taken over. It was an opportunity to make sure that the Magpie Police Service had the same standards as other police departments in the country.

Lillian ran to her Tahoe with a speed and agility that hadn't been present when she'd arrived. She climbed into her SUV and reversed out of the driveway as if she were trying to escape a fire. George didn't blame her for beating a hasty retreat. If she could run away from her life, she would. But if the situation was reversed and she was visiting a friend who'd lost their license, she would've offered them a ride or asked if they needed help. Not that she was in the mood for company, but the offer would've been nice.

She glanced around her house. Maybe her place did look messy. The trouble was, she had a hard time throwing things away. There was always a short pile of newspaper next to the fireplace to use as kindling. Her kitchen cupboards held an assortment of empty, cleaned food containers, and there were stacks of canned foods in the pantry—just in case.

George lifted the plastic wrap from the paper plate Lillian had given her and sniffed the cookies. Peanut butter. The smell turned her stomach as it always did. She couldn't eat them, but maybe Smokey would like them. She went to the kitchen and grabbed a tub that had once held Margarine, tipped the cookies in, and snapped on the lid. Then she added them to her backpack and headed out.

CHAPTER SEVEN

The walk took George longer than anticipated, but it was pleasant enough. There was a dirt track that followed the lake into town. She spotted loons diving for food in the deeper water. A family of ducks, possibly mallards, swam by. They stayed in the safety of the reeds by the shore. A single magpie with its distinctive black and white plumage swooped in front of her, flying from a maple to a spruce tree. An old English superstition about magpies sprang to mind.

One for sorrow
Two for joy
Three for a girl
Four for a boy
Five for Silver
Six for gold
Seven for a secret never to be told.

Her maternal grandmother had been British and had taught her mother, Tina, the rhyme. In her darkest moments, Tina had taken the verse as fact. If one magpie had flown in front of her, she would've gone back to bed, convinced her day would be a disaster.

How different would George's upbringing have been if Hank hadn't robbed her mother of her ability to function? His need to control Tina with drugs and his ability to convince her that her feelings and observations weren't real had made Tina question her sanity and had led to a breakdown.

Poplar tree fuzz drifted on the breeze. As a child, George had tried to catch the floating seeds and make a wish, believing they were fairies. Another of Tina's folk stories. It was one of the few magical memories George had of her mother. With Tina sick, George had been forced to care for Grace. Looking after her sister hadn't been a burden, but it would've been nice to have a carefree childhood.

Like most busy people, she drove everywhere because it was faster. Normally, she took the car to the gym and to work. After her shift, she was so tired she would take a hot bath, stream a show on her laptop, read a book, and sleep. On her days off, she stocked up on groceries, cleaned her house, and ran errands. Who had time to walk? As of today, she did, which was good because it gave her time to enjoy the moment. *That's right, make the most of it.*

An older couple nodded hello as they passed her on the trail and then continued chatting. They seemed to have a familiarity that came from years of togetherness. A wave of yearning rose unbidden. She'd seen that connection with other couples but had never experienced it herself. She'd had two relationships in college but both had fizzled out, not that they'd ever been that hot to begin with. She hadn't been upset when they'd ended because neither boyfriend had mattered that much.

An image of Liam with his dark, intense eyes, athletic build, and cheeky grin sprang to mind. She smiled at her own stupidity. No man would want to get involved with a woman who was in the middle of a crisis. And she wasn't the type of woman who slept around. For her, sex was intimate, and although her past relationships hadn't been passionate, they had been exclusive.

She came to Smokey's old, rundown cabin, which in her opinion was beyond repair and should be torn down. The front porch sagged dangerously. Paint was no longer peeling from the window frames because it had worn off completely, and the moss-covered roofing tiles either curled or were missing altogether.

As always, there was the faint smell of a campfire. The place looked deserted, which worked in her favor. She wasn't in the mood to talk. She left the container of cookies on his doorstep with a note and headed back to the trail and her thoughts.

Her life was a mess. She needed to take one day at a time. Once the tests were done, she would know what to expect in the future. She wished Doctor Sullivan had written down the information instead of simply telling her. At the time, she'd been so shocked she hadn't been able to take it all in. She didn't even know the names of the examinations or what to expect. She knew the doctor had ordered them and that she would probably get a phone call or a letter informing her of where and when to appear for her appointments, but that was it. It all felt so unstable, as if the floor were shifting beneath her.

She had no idea how an epilepsy diagnosis would affect her work. Best case scenario, the chief would put her on desk duty. Worst case, she would be out of a job.

For years, Grace had been telling her to leave Magpie in the past and get on with her life. But somehow George hadn't been able to walk away. Had she been fooling herself into believing that her work as a community cop improved the lives of the people of Magpie? And her efforts somehow mitigated the damaged done by her father? Or maybe she wanted revenge for all the hurt Hank had caused. At this point, she wasn't certain of anything and wasn't sure any of it mattered because she'd failed. Hank wasn't in jail, and as far as she knew, there were no ongoing investigations into his activities.

The dirt trail turned to paved road at the Magpie Sports and Community center, which housed an indoor swimming pool, a gym, a skating rink, and rooms large enough for classes and meetings. Her view widened as she approached Lakeshore Drive and left the cover of the trees. There were several boats and Sea-Doos on the lake. A dad with his two children bobbed in their aluminum fishing boat about five hundred yards from the shore.

Heat shimmered off the road even though it was still early. Sweat dribbled down her back. An iced coffee would be just the thing to cool her down. She would've preferred to go to the café attached to the Charm Hotel, but that was up by the highway, and she didn't want to walk that far with the temperature climbing. She passed the Chinese restaurant and headed for the Jumping Bean coffee shop next door. She'd ignore Mrs. King's obvious disdain, grab a drink, and sit in the shade of an umbrella on the deck.

CHAPTER EIGHT

After the quiet walk, the sights and sounds of the town were overwhelming. The streets were packed with tourists. Most were carrying towels, floaties, and other sun gear and seemed to be headed for the beach.

She sighed with relief as she entered the air-conditioned interior of the Jumping Bean. Mrs. King, the mayor's wife, frowned at her as she joined the line to order her drink. The sophisticated older woman had the polished look of a model and could've graced the cover of a senior's fashion magazine. Her clothes were simple and chic. Her gray hair was cut into stylish, shoulder-length layers. She had never smiled at George, not once, and today was no exception.

George couldn't think of any reason for Mrs. King's hostility. Most people in town had overcome their preconceived notions about her and her connection to Hank, but not Mrs. King. At the first glimpse of her, Mrs. King made a face as though she'd just gotten a whiff of a bad fart. It was something George had learned to live with.

She ordered a mocha frappe, all the while ignoring the older woman's contempt. The overly sweet beverage topped with whipped cream and dripping with chocolate syrup was an indulgence. But she figured with everything going on, she deserved a little decadence. Once her order was ready, she headed outside away from Mrs. King's scowl. She found a free table on the deck under the shade of an umbrella where she could watch the comings and goings on the street.

A tall, handsome man with brown hair who was in need of a shave stopped in front of her and smiled as if waiting for her to acknowledge his presence.

It took her a moment to recognize him. "John?" She rose out of her chair and hugged him. "How are you? What's it been? Eight years?"

As a teen, she'd seen John Rogers, Mattie's son, as a cool, handsome, older brother. With his good looks and athletic ability, it seemed only natural he would receive a scholarship and go off to university to play football. Unfortunately, he had been injured in his second year of college and hadn't completed his degree. After that, she'd lost touch with him.

He smiled down at her, seeming as easygoing as ever. "Yeah, something like that. I heard you made good and became a cop."

Talking about her work felt like pouring vinegar in her eyes so she changed the subject. "Mattie said you were hurt playing football. What are you doing now?"

He fished a card from his pocket and handed it to her. "I'm into real estate and flipping a few properties." His voice had a nasal quality as if he had a cold.

"I'm glad to hear you're doing well. Mattie worries about you." George stuffed the card into her pocket, knowing she wouldn't need it.

John frowned, and his hands fisted by his sides. "She worries too much. She's always been the overbearing motherly type." His jaw was clenched so tight he seemed to have trouble talking. In less than two seconds, his demeanor had changed from carefree to angry.

"I'm grateful for her mothering instinct." As a teen, George and Grace had spent countless hours in Mattie's storeroom hiding from their father. Mattie was the only person they could count on. If they needed help, she was there. She'd given them food, shelter, and encouraged them to do well in school.

John smiled again, his foul mood apparently evaporating. The fingers of his left hand tapped a rhythm against his thigh. "Things are going really well for me. I just moved back to town. I have a place on River Road."

Something about him was off. His short brown hair was messy and stuck up in spikes as though he'd just climbed out of bed and forgotten to comb it. She remembered him as being neat and careful with his appearance. He'd also had the most vivid

45

blue eyes, but now they seemed almost black in color.

"I should get some coffee." When he smiled, she realized the reason his blue eyes looked dark was because his pupils were enlarged. That wouldn't mean much in a dim room, but the sun was beating down on them, making her squint.

"Take care." She sat down and took another sip of her icy coffee, being sure not to look at him.

She took her smartphone out of her backpack and searched for signs of narcotic addiction. He didn't have all the symptoms listed on the website, but there could be a case made for anxiety, irritability, nasal stuffiness, and his huge pupils.

She pretended to be texting as she watched John exit the building and walk down the street.

A bad bout of the flu could also account for his symptoms, but John had been injured playing football. He could've gotten addicted to pain killers. Mattie had told George that John was married and lived in Calgary. That obviously wasn't the case anymore, and he hadn't mentioned a wife.

But they'd only had a two-minute conversation. She was probably wrong about him. Conjuring up problems for other people was a way for her to forget her own difficulties, but she'd have a quiet word with Mattie all the same.

A family rode by on bikes. She recognized the bright blue frames as those rented by Buddy. He was another childhood friend who could best be described as a jack-of-all-trades and a mechanical genius who could fix anything. One of his trades was bike rental. Having wheels, even the pedaling kind, would make her life easier. She grabbed her coffee and headed toward Magpie Marine Repair and Sales on River Road. Buddy ran his business out of a small corner of the repair shop.

She slowed to a stroll as she passed the Credit and Savings Bank. The cooling effects of her coffee had worn off so that sweat collected at her temples and a bead of moisture dribbled down the side of her face. She stopped under a small ash tree that was part of the bank landscaping and wiped it away.

The newer structure and parking lot sat on the corner of the lake and the river, filling the block of River Road that stretched from Lakeshore Drive and Main Street. It was an ugly, art deco style office building that serviced not only the town, but everyone in the surrounding area. The planners had done a good job positioning the structure next to the river so there were plenty of parking spaces for their patrons at the front.

In the winter, they were open regular office hours but now, when the summer season brought campers and other tourists looking to enjoy watersports on the lake, they stayed open until nine in the evening.

The bank must've hired a bunch of landscapers to clean up their lot. There were six men, all of them wearing jeans, a yellow safety vest, safety goggles, and painter's masks. One was sweeping the sidewalk in front of the building. Two were trimming the bushes. The other three were standing around, seemingly waiting for orders.

She stepped out from under the shade of the tree and set a steady pace. By the time she reached Magpie Marine Repair and Sales, she was sweating again.

George sighed with relief as she entered the cool air-conditioned office. She wrinkled her nose at the smell of oil and old engines.

"He's not here," the young blond woman behind the counter announced before George could say anything.

"Will he be long?"

The blond shook her head, her long hair swaying with the movement. "He didn't say."

"Can you give him a message? Can you tell him that George needs to rent a bike?"

"Hey, aren't you the cop that had a fit in the Charm Hotel?" she said as she scribbled George's name on a piece of paper.

George's cheeks burned with embarrassment. She sprinted for the door, unable to reply. Why hadn't she anticipated answering questions about her condition? She'd always pictured herself as a strong, independent woman who could hold her own in any situation. But a misfiring in her brain had laid her low and

47

changed her life. Whether that change was temporary or permanent she didn't know.

CHAPTER NINE

George reached the sidewalk on River Road, took a calming breath, and focused her mind. Ducks screeched with their raucous quacking on the river to her right. A breeze picked up, coming off the lake straight ahead, making the heat bearable. Cars roared by on the road to her left.

Maybe walking into town hadn't been her best idea. She hadn't counted on her situation being common knowledge, which was stupid of her because she'd passed out in a public place. There was no hiding from the truth or the emotions that came with it. She should have been prepared for the reactions, and it had been naïve of her not to take it into account.

But there was no need to panic. Her work as a community cop meant she was well-known. It was natural for people to be curious. The next time someone asked her about the incident, she would tell them she was waiting for tests. There, she had a plan. *Deal with the now.*

She backtracked along River Road, heading toward the bank. Allowing herself to wallow in self-pity wasn't going to do any good. She needed to get a grip. What did it matter if she had to move and change careers? It wasn't like when she was a kid and at the mercy of her father. She was an adult. Not being able to drive didn't mean she couldn't still work for the greater good. It just meant her vision of her future would change.

She was so caught up in her thoughts that she almost stepped in front of an armored truck as it turned into the bank parking lot. The driver slammed on his brakes. She waved, mouthed the word "sorry," and then stepped back on the sidewalk, allowing them to continue.

As the vehicle pulled up to the door, one of the landscapers threw down his rake and marched toward the armored vehicle.

From her position on the pathway, George could see him

reach into his pocket. He pulled out a small black canister.

The two guards ignored him as they opened the back door of their truck.

"Look out," she screamed as she started running.

The gardener charged the guards, spraying each of them in the face. Then he grabbed two money bags and ran.

George sprinted toward the crime in progress, wishing she was wearing her police radio so she could call for backup.

The perpetrator ran through the parking lot and rounded the corner, heading to the rear of the building. He was incredibly fast. Her heart pounded as she raced, trying to catch up with the thief.

A bright orange muscle car screeched into a parking spot at the side of the building, coming to a halt right in front of her. She slammed into it, fell backward, and landed in a heap on the sidewalk.

"Jeez, lady, look where you're going," the driver shouted through his open window.

She rolled to a sitting position, breathing heavily. "I'm a cop. There's been a robbery." Ignoring the ache in her lower back, she stood and shuffled to the rear of the bank, but the thief seemed to have vanished.

The driver, who was in his late thirties, climbed out of his vehicle and followed her. "You're paying for the damage to my car." He had a scruffy beard and wore sunglasses, a tank top, and shorts. Everything about him, including the way he shouted at her, screamed entitlement.

"Did you get a look at the guy I was chasing? He robbed an armored truck." She ignored his outrage and walked back toward the scene of the heist, dismissing the fact that she hurt from head to toe.

He raced to block her path and screamed into her face, "You dented my car!"

She'd had enough of his belligerent attitude. "You were driving too fast in a parking lot and hit a cop in pursuit of a suspect. You will probably be charged with dangerous driving."

As if responding on cue, sirens sounded in the distance. Magpie was a small town, and George estimated the police service would arrive in less than a minute. She paced to the rear of his vehicle, memorizing his license plate in case he decided not to wait around.

Muscle Car Guy paled. "What?"

George waved him toward the front of the bank. "I'm sure the officers will want to talk to you. Let's go. You can give them a statement."

He led the way, seemingly resigned to his fate.

A crowd had gathered around the guards who sat at the rear of the truck. A woman George recognized as a bank teller used a bottle of water to flush the younger guards' eyes.

George joined them. The older of the two security men held his face, cursing.

"Are you okay?" She bent down, checking both men. There didn't seem to be any fatal injuries. Neither of the men were struggling to breathe. Although they were in some discomfort, they seemed to be coping physically.

The young guard coughed, his face an unnatural shade of pink. "We're fine."

A Magpie Police Service SUV squealed to a halt next to the armored truck, with Liam behind the wheel. He jumped out and walked toward the crime scene, moving with a supple grace. His police uniform made him seem even more masculine, which she hadn't thought was possible.

George's stomach did a little flip, reminding her that she was not immune to him. She waved, letting him know she was there, and then sat on the sidewalk in the shade of a small maple. A slight tremor quivered through her body and her knees felt weak, probably a reaction to the adrenaline crash. It seemed every time Liam was in the vicinity, she was hurt or beat up. The man was her own personal, sexy bad-luck charm.

CHAPTER TEN

Chief Evans arrived along with other members of the Magpie Police Service. Liam let them take over the scene. Catching the perpetrator who had committed the robbery wasn't on his to-do list.

Georgina sat on the sidewalk with her knees hugged to her chest, looking like a wild woman who'd gone a couple of rounds with a prize fighter and lost. Her eyes looked silver today.

She probably hadn't recovered from her seizure, and here she was, again, involved in a situation where she could've been injured.

"I'm tempted to take you home and tie you to your bed," he said as he approached.

"Pardon me?" She gave him a look that suggested he'd lost his mind.

Only then did he realize what he'd said. "I meant, you seem to attract trouble." Heat flooded his cheeks. "I didn't mean…" He sighed. "I've only known you a few days. In that time, you've been knocked unconscious, had a seizure, and now this. It's hard to see you hurting every time we meet."

"Yes, and I hold you fully responsible. My life was uneventful until you showed up." She grinned, letting him know she was joking.

His throat felt too thick to answer as he pictured the moment her head hit the pavement just a few short days ago.

She continued talking as if sensing his unease. "I had to come into town because I need food. I didn't plan any of this." Her hand shook as she wiped a bead of sweat from her brow. Her statement seemed honest, reasonable, and understandable.

"Can you tell me what happened?" Liam pulled his notebook from his pocket, pretending to care about the theft.

Her long dark hair hung about her face in an unruly mess.

He imagined this was how she'd look after a night of lovemaking, except without the dazed, beaten look in her eyes. He shook away the thought and focused on his fake job.

She stopped talking and stared at him, obviously waiting for an answer.

Damn. He'd allowed his physical attraction to distract him and hadn't paid attention to what she was saying. After a moment's silence, he thought of a question. "You said there were six landscapers?"

"Yes, and he was one of them." She shrugged. "I assume the bank hired them."

"Maybe you can show me the route the perpetrator took when you chased him."

She eased to a standing position. "Sure." Her quivering extended to her whole body.

He was amazed she was able to stay upright. It spoke of her inner strength and her selflessness that she was still prepared to help despite everything that had happened.

"He ran to the side of the bank. The last I saw he was heading this way." She rounded the corner of the building. There were a couple of parking spots at the side, one of them filled with a bright orange Mustang.

He pointed to the car, which was well-kept and was obviously someone's summer toy. A rear-wheel drive vehicle was no good on Alberta's winter roads. "Is this the car that hit you?"

She winced. "Actually, I hit the car. The driver sped into the parking spot and stopped in front of me. I couldn't brake fast enough." She rubbed her backside. It was an unconscious movement and a reminder that her butt still hurt from when she'd hit the pavement.

"Do you think our landscaper had a getaway vehicle waiting at the rear of the bank?" The geography of the area meant the culprit would've had very few options when it came to making his escape because the building backed onto a grass embankment and then the river.

She tilted her head to one side as she considered the options.

53

"Anything's possible, but I think I would've noticed if a car had passed me. And I have to wonder if this was a crime of opportunity or if it was planned. He could have headed this way just to get away from me." Her eyes narrowed.

"What is it?" he prompted.

"It was planned." She nodded as if confirming some unasked question. "Why else would he have pepper spray?"

"You think he took this route deliberately." He liked watching her puzzle through the crime.

She walked around the Mustang and made her way to the grass verge that edged the river.

She turned her gaze south toward the lake and then north downstream, taking in the river and the bridge, the same bridge where they'd apprehended Naked Nick just a few days ago. "I didn't see a car go past me, but maybe I was distracted by the driver of the Mustang."

"It's low-traffic. I would've thought you'd notice."

She shrugged and stared at the dark, rippling water. "He could've run along the grass embankment and headed for the highway."

The vegetation was mowed in places, but it was also peppered with low-growing bushes and tall weeds and could never be described as a trail. She took a few steps toward the bridge. "I don't think…" She pointed to a dogwood, its pretty pink flowers blooming. "What's that?"

A piece of white poked out between the dandelions and the shrubs.

George held up her hands, indicating she wasn't going to touch anything and inched closer. She stopped six feet away. "You need to see this."

He followed her footsteps. A bright yellow safety vest, a cap, a painter's mask, and a pair of goggles were strewn on the ground next to the water. Because of the steep incline, they weren't readily visible from the parking lot.

Liam let out a low whistle. "I'll be damned." The disguise had been discarded in a haphazard manner.

"He took a risk." Georgina shaded her eyes with her hand as she scanned the water.

"How do you mean?"

"He either swam or walked along the river. Maybe he had a car waiting near the bridge. She backed away, carefully, leaving the crime scene untouched. "There are traffic cameras on the bridge. There'll be a record if he went that way." She took another step and slipped on the uneven ground.

He caught her around the waist. She stared up at him and, once again, he was lost. Her dark hair, light eyes, her smooth skin, her tall, slim figure and the innocent way she looked at him were all at odds with everything he'd been led to believe. Her file hadn't mentioned any boyfriends or lovers. But a woman this attractive couldn't possibly be unattached. Had her background taught her how to seduce men? Was playing innocent one of her weapons? He would have to be on his guard.

She stepped out of his arms, apparently recovering her composure. "Sorry."

He cleared his throat. "He could've just had a boat waiting and sailed out onto the lake. There are tons of places where he could've parked a getaway vehicle along the lakeshore."

She straightened, as if standing tall gave her focus. "He could've. But that's not what I would do."

"Not what you would do?" He was surprised by the way she phrased her answer. As though she planned armored car heists on a regular basis.

She shrugged, ignoring his obvious shock at her admission. "There are a lot of people on the lake today. Families, people on jet skis, all relaxing, having a good time. Someone in a rush would be noticed. But I could be wrong. Maybe he has nerves of steel and is out there pretending to relax and enjoy the sun."

"What are you saying?"

"I didn't see him once I hit the car." She frowned, causing a small vertical line to appear between her eyebrows. "I could be wrong about the riverbank. The marine shop has access to the river. He'd have to go past them. Everything after seeing him run to the back of the building is conjecture on my part."

He liked that she'd seen the flaw in her statement. She wasn't like any woman he'd ever known. She seemed completely unaware of her beauty and gave the impression that the community of Magpie was important to her. Maybe part of her wanted to be a real cop.

That was something he could exploit. They could work the investigation together. It would be an excellent way to get close to her. Normally, investigations were compartmentalized. Only the officers involved discussed the case. He was about to break that rule. The chief wouldn't like it, but Liam wasn't going to ask permission.

CHAPTER ELEVEN

Georgina tried not to look at Liam as they walked back to the armored car. The man was a lodestone. When he'd caught her to prevent her from falling, it was as if every molecule in her body had come alive. She just hoped she wasn't staring at him like a twelve-year-old with a crush. Her mouth watered at the thought of kissing him. Heat flooded her body and she licked her lips.

"She did what?" Chief Evans roared as he levered himself out of the cruiser.

She swallowed hard. Her throat was suddenly dry. He glared, his expression cold and hard as he stomped toward her. "Did I hear right? You pursued the suspect? Why would you do that when you're off duty?" he shouted.

She could feel the gaze of the other officers, the medics, and the people in the crowd on her. Her cheeks burned, scorching from her public humiliation. She took a step back and turned away from him, desperately trying to bury her anger. Her hands balled into fists. Her father had used this tactic to control her when she was a child. There was no way she would tolerate it as an adult. She swung around to face him, not willing to accept verbal abuse from another bully.

Liam stepped between them. "With all due respect sir, I would appreciate it if you would lower your voice." He faced Evans with his back to her so she couldn't see his expression.

"Why the hell...?" Chief Evans scanned the bystanders then cleared his throat. He sidestepped Liam, and in a measured tone said, "Tell me why you raced after the suspect."

Liam positioned himself to the side like a referee in a boxing match.

"I might be off duty, but I was hoping to get a license plate or a description...something that would help us apprehend him."

The chief scowled as he assessed her. He didn't say anything for a long time. Instead, he towered over her as if he could intimidate her with his greater size. What he saw she couldn't say, but his dislike for her was becoming more apparent with each encounter. She was grateful Liam had intervened. If he hadn't, things could have gotten ugly, and then it might not matter if she had a driver's license or not. She would have argued herself right out of a job.

Liam broke the silence. "We found his clothing down by the river. It seems that he used the stream or the riverbank to make his escape."

The chief nodded. "He got away with hundreds of thousands of dollars. I've put in a call to the RCMP. They'll take over the case. You can give them your report."

That made sense. A small community operation like the Magpie Police Service didn't have the resources or the manpower to work this sort of investigation.

"Yes, sir." Liam met the chief's gaze. It almost seemed as though the two men were engaged in some unspoken communication.

An RCMP police cruiser with its sirens blaring pulled into the parking lot.

Liam went to greet them, smiling as he shook hands with a blond female officer who looked to be in her forties. She wore the standard RCMP uniform, which included navy pants with a yellow strip and a starched shirt under a bullet-proof vest that had the word POLICE emblazoned on the front in bold white letters. The badge on her upper arm near her shoulder indicated she was a sergeant.

"And you, young lady." The chief turned his attention to her. "Go home and stay there."

"Sir, I have done nothing to justify being placed under house arrest and refuse to be imprisoned in my own home." She softened her tone, hoping to sound less combative. "I need to be able to walk into town. I have no other way of getting food and necessities."

He rolled his eyes, his lack of respect apparent. "Okay. Just stay home for the rest of the day."

Without another word, she ducked under the crime scene tape and headed up Main Street. She'd grab whatever she needed from the supermarket and then head to her house. Normally, she would've stayed and made a report to the RCMP, but there was no way she could remain in the chief's company and control her temper. He had pushed her buttons. Given everything that had happened in the last few days, she doubted she would be able to restrain herself. Liam had her contact details. He could give them to the Mounties.

This past week was the worst she'd experienced in a long time. The war she was fighting with Hank was going nowhere. At least when Chief Hunt had been in charge, he'd tried to put her father away, but as far as she could tell, nothing good had come of the change of command in the Magpie Police Service.

The only bright spot was Liam. She'd been avoiding making any emotional connections for a long time and had no idea why. She was in danger of becoming a lonely, bitter woman. Maybe it was time to take a chance and trust someone. What did she have to lose?

CHAPTER TWELVE

George slammed her laptop shut, stood, and stretched. She'd taken a couple of aspirin, soaked in a hot bath, and then rested while strategically placing ice packs on the worst of her bruises. Streaming videos on the internet had done nothing to distract her from the events of the day.

She paced to her living room window. The sun was low in the western sky. A thunderstorm was forecast for later that night, and she could see clouds far away on the southern horizon. Long sunsets were normal this time of year. As they approached midsummer, the sun didn't set until after ten, and nights didn't get completely dark. It was more like a long twilight. A reminder that in the Arctic, just over sixteen hundred miles away, it was light twenty-four hours a day.

"Well, today sucked." She wasn't sure what had shaken her more: witnessing the robbery and hitting the car, or her encounter with chief Evans. She rubbed her still-sore butt. There was no doubt her body and soul had taken a beating in the last few days.

She would love to be able to talk to her sister, Grace. She'd even pulled up Grace's contact on her smartphone but had stopped shy of dialing the number. Although her sister hadn't said anything, George suspected Grace's relationship with her boyfriend, Rob, had hit a rocky patch. This holiday was important to them, and George didn't want to bother them with her problems.

Plus, Grace might not be too sympathetic. As far as her sister was concerned, George's fixation with getting justice and seeing Hank behind bars was unhealthy. But how could she walk away when she knew Hank was out there? Grace and Tina had changed their last names but were still terrified he would track them down and hurt them. Being constantly afraid was no way to live.

A walk along the lakeshore might be just what she needed to work off some of her nervous energy. As she laced up her runners, the doorbell rang.

She peered through the ornamental window in the front door and then opened it wide. "Buddy, it's good to see you."

Even though Buddy, whose real name was Andrew Mackenzie, was now tall, athletic, and good looking with a nice smile, in her mind, he would always be the fat kid in school who'd been bullied.

"I heard you came by." He grinned, his easy-going nature shining through.

She stepped aside, allowing him entry. "Yeah, I was wondering if I could rent a bike from you."

He slipped off his flip flops and plopped down on her couch. "Sure, how long do you need it for?" He wore a pair of khaki shorts and a white T-shirt with not a smudge of oil in sight. These were stylish clothes for him.

She shrugged. "I don't know."

His gaze softened. "I heard what happened."

She made her way to the armchair adjacent to the couch, not wanting to see the sympathy in his eyes. It was bad enough hearing it in his voice.

"George. It's okay. It's actually nice to know you're as human as the rest of us."

Finally, she focused on him and was surprised to find him laughing. "You bastard! You're enjoying this." She picked up a decorative cushion and threw it at his head.

He grimaced as he caught it. "Not really, but you don't always have to be the tough one. I can fight my own battles now, and so can everyone else."

"I didn't fight because you were weak. I did it because that's what friends do."

"And a friend would lend you a bike. I won't rent it to you."

She nodded. It was a kind gesture and one she couldn't refuse, not without insulting him.

He stood and shuffled into his flip flops. "I have one in the back of my truck."

She followed him out and watched as he opened the tailgate of his newer Ford pickup.

He easily hoisted the bike up the steps onto her deck, where he leaned it against the railing.

"Here's a bike lock." He shoved the D-shaped device and the key into her hand. "Use it."

"I'm a cop. Of course I'll use it."

"You'll need a helmet. They have an ugly selection at the hardware store."

"I'll get one first thing tomorrow."

He smiled and waved as he headed for the driver's door. "Keep it as long as you need it."

"Are you in a rush? I thought we could…"

He shook his head. "Can't. I've got a hot date with a woman from Calgary."

George smiled. As much as she would've liked to spend time with her old friend, it was good to hear he was enjoying himself. "Is she on holiday, looking to have some fun?"

"I hope so." His grin widened as he climbed into his truck.

George waved as she watched him leave, then closed her front door and gingerly inched down onto her couch with her laptop in her hand. She was glad Buddy's arrival had stopped her from going for a walk. She was way too sore from the day's activities. She'd shop for a bike helmet online and then maybe take another bath.

She'd just opened her computer when her doorbell rang again.

She groaned, not wanting to move.

The doorbell buzzed again, followed by knocking.

"Hang on. I'm coming," she snapped as she eased to a standing position.

She ground her teeth as the bell rang for a third time.

Slowly, so as not to aggravate her sore butt, she made her way to the door. She peered through the window to find Liam's dark eyes staring back at her.

"What the hell?" she said as she opened the door.

"Nice place you've got here." He barged in, filling her small living room. "Was that Buddy, aka Andrew Mackenzie, I saw leaving?"

"He's an old friend. He lent me a bike so I can get around." She narrowed her eyes and fisted her palms. Liam had forced his way into her home in the same way she would've when interviewing a suspect.

"Nice place." He scanned her house.

"You already said that." She was beyond caring whether it was tidy enough or good enough. Her world was crashing down in slow motion, and she wasn't in the mood to deal with any crap. "You need to tell me why you're here...*now*."

He smiled at her again, his dark eyes shining. "Didn't I say?"

Her patience was at an end. "Get to the point or leave."

"Sorry." He shook his head. "I want to invite you to coffee tomorrow morning."

"Why?" Everything about this was wrong.

"Because we're friends and—"

"Cut the bullshit." She poked him in the chest. "You just forced your way into my house as if I'd done something wrong. I'm going to give you one chance to tell me what that's all about, and then you can leave."

His gaze traveled from her feet to her head. She felt like an insect under a magnifying glass. Finally, after a long moment of silence, he said, "Buddy is working for your father."

"No." George stepped back, her hand covering her mouth. "That can't be true."

"That's our intelligence."

"But he knows how bad it was. He used to share his lunch with us."

"Us?"

"Me and Grace. He's one of the good guys. How could he?" She stopped and stared at Liam. "How do you have this information? You're a rookie. Why have you been given access while the rest of us are in the dark."

He shrugged, seemingly unfazed. "The chief told me today. Apparently, a citizen came forward. I was told to be on the look-out. I'm sure you would've been told if you weren't on leave."

She sighed. That all seemed reasonable. Her time off could still be measured in hours, and she was already out of the loop.

His gaze softened. "Why was he here?"

"I told you. He lent me a bike." She opened the door and walked out onto her small deck. The bike, which was painted bright blue, sat chained to a railing. "Do you think I should give it back?"

"Keep it for now. I'll talk to the chief on your behalf and let him know. You don't want to arouse Buddy's suspicions."

Her stomach heaved. She pictured her childhood friend. His carefree demeanor was just an illusion. In reality, he was in trouble and would probably end up in jail. Another casualty of her father.

"Are you okay?" Liam stood by her side, tall and solid.

"I'm just having a bad day." How did she explain her devastation at this latest blow? "I would really like to be left alone now."

His dark eyes bored into her. What he saw, she couldn't say and didn't care. "I need you to leave."

"That's blunt."

"As blunt as you barging your way into my home," she countered, still not prepared to put up with his shit.

He scrubbed a hand over his face. "You're right. Seeing Buddy triggered a protective reaction. I lost my head."

"Protective reaction?" She stood toe to toe with him. "I don't need you or anyone else to protect me."

He took a step back, putting some distance between them. "I shouldn't have made a big deal out of it."

"You think?"

"Let me buy you a coffee as an apology." He didn't look sorry. He seemed relaxed and comfortable. Her obvious fury hadn't affected him at all.

She should tell him she was busy, but what if she was the one overreacting? She was out of sorts. The emotional upheaval from the last couple of days could be affecting her judgement. Lashing out at Liam would be an easy way for her to release some tension, but he had protected her from Chief Evans earlier today, so maybe she could cut him some slack.

Finally, she nodded her agreement. "Okay, but I could do with some alone time right now."

He nodded. "How about I pick you up at ten tomorrow?"

He had the most mesmerizing eyes. His irises seemed to blend into his pupils like pools of dark melted chocolate.

Finally, she realized he was staring at her, waiting for an answer. "Ten is fine. Bye." She went inside and closed the door, not waiting for him to leave.

She had no enthusiasm for their coffee date. In fact, she wasn't even sure if going was a good idea. He didn't trust her, that was evident. Was he suspicious of her because of her history or because of Buddy? If Buddy was in trouble, then she had to find a way to help him. But how could she do that when her own life was in such a mess?

CHAPTER THIRTEEN

Georgina hadn't spoken on the short drive to the Jumping Bean coffee shop. Liam wasn't sure if that was in character for her or not. He'd met her only a few hours before she'd been knocked unconscious. All his interactions with her had revolved around her work as a community police officer. He didn't know her personally and had no idea who she really was. He'd made suppositions, which had been determined by the reports he'd read when preparing for this assignment, but it had become apparent that her file was incomplete.

Seeming stiff, she eased out of the truck as soon as he came to a stop. She was probably feeling the effects of hitting the Mustang yesterday. She waited for him on the sidewalk.

Holy shit. She was hot. She wore a pair of shorts, which looked like a cutoff pair of jeans, and a black tank top. The outfit accentuated her long legs and the contours of her body. It was something he didn't want to notice. He didn't want to be attracted to her, or ache to touch her. On a physical level, everything about her excited him, which was all the proof he needed to know that his dick had a mind of its own, especially when it reacted to errant pheromones for no logical reason.

She arched her back as she stretched. The movement drew him in, making him notice her flat stomach and the curve of her small breasts. She straightened and faced the coffee shop. He curled his hands into fists as he stared at her perfectly round behind. *Fuck.* Chemistry was a bitch.

She swung back to face him. "This is a nice truck."

He eyed his Dodge Ram as he joined her, burying his attraction. "It's seven years old. My parents gave it to me when they still approved of my lifestyle."

"Wow, they gave you a truck. I thought that only happened in movies. That means your parents are rich." She eyed the vehicle.

He couldn't seem to lie to her, which was strange. This had never happened before. But he hadn't said anything, so far, that would compromise the investigation. He'd just adapt and stick to his real life as a backstory. It was easier to remember anyway. "Yeah, I guess. Although, we're not on good terms anymore, which means they're still rich, but I'm not."

She frowned, nodded, and took off without him, heading for the café. He was surprised she hadn't commented on the state of his relationship with his family. Maybe she didn't consider it a big deal when compared to her situation.

He caught up with her and grabbed her elbow, forcing her to face him. "Are you in a hurry?"

"No, I'm just...I'm...To be honest, I don't know what I'm doing here."

"You don't want to spend time with me because your problems started when I tackled you." That wasn't true. Her problems started when she stole drugs from the evidence locker, but he'd play along.

"No." Her gaze connected with his. "I'm just a little off kilter, that's all. I need to find some balance."

He could sense her seriousness. "And how do you do that?"

"Stop wallowing, of course." She gave him a bright smile that kicked him in the gut. How could someone who seemed to be so good work for a criminal?

The interior of the Jumping Bean was quiet. There were just a few customers sitting at wrought iron tables that were topped with frosted glass.

Liam guided her to a vacant seat near the window. "What can I get for you?"

"A plain coffee frappé."

Mrs. King smiled at him as he approached the counter. "Hi. Do you want your usual, black coffee with room for cream?"

"Sure." He smiled back. "Did you get a new haircut? It looks good."

The polished older woman had her gray shoulder-length hair styled. Liam couldn't have said what kind of cut it was, and he didn't care. In his experience, any woman who took the time to apply makeup, paint her nails, and do her hair wanted to be noticed and complimented.

Mrs. King blushed in response. "It's nice of you to say so."

He waited for their drinks and then joined Georgina as she gazed out of the window. Her skin had honey-colored sheen. Her complexion and her dark hair contrasted with her light eyes. She brushed a strand of hair away from her face, making him notice her fighter's hands. Her knuckles were scarred and larger than they should be. It was a reminder that this beautifully exotic woman was no delicate damsel, waiting for a knight to save her.

She frowned at him, leaned over, and whispered, "What's with the fake charm?"

"Fake? Women like my charm. It's not fake." His heart thudded hard in his chest at the thought that she had seen through his undercover persona.

"Yes, it is. You're pretending to be nice, and it's creepy."

He inwardly sighed in relief. She was just criticizing his personality. "No, it's not." He was undercover. Everything about him was pretend except his charisma.

"Perhaps it's me." She shrugged. "Hank knows how to win people over when it suits him. As far as I'm concerned, charm is a veneer people use to hide who they really are."

He stared at her for a moment, wondering if that was true of everyone and not just her criminal father. He decided to change the subject and pointed to a well-toned, shirtless man with a guitar slung across his back, waiting for his coffee. "Could he have pulled off the robbery yesterday?"

She craned her neck to get a good look at him.

Good. She'd taken the bait. He wanted to talk about the robbery and distract her from the way he'd angered her last night. If he could gain her trust in one part of her life, then maybe she would confide in him about other aspects, too.

"No, that's Ralph, otherwise known as Shirtless Guitar Guy. He performs on the beach. He's too broad in the shoulders. The guy we're looking for has a slim build. Although, I can't shake the feeling that I know him. There was something familiar about him."

"You think it's someone you know?" he said, repeating her statement. "That's a gamble. What if he was recognized? But I guess four-hundred thousand was worth the risk."

"Four-hundred thousand?" She stared at him with her mouth open and then said, "Holy cow."

"And the landscapers..." He paused, ensuring he had her attention. "They were not employed by the bank."

"They weren't?" Her voice rose. She realized she was too loud and covered her mouth.

"No, all five of them were hired through an online ad. They had to bring their own vest, gardening equipment, cap, goggles and painters masks, and then at the end of the day they were to report to the cashier's window and get two hundred bucks."

"But they're out of money because there was no job. It was all a setup."

"Exactly."

"They were just there to distract from the one landscaper who was the thief." She poked the air as she talked.

He nodded. "And the online ad is untraceable."

She closed her lips around the straw and took a sip of her coffee. It was the most erotic thing he'd ever seen. He hadn't realized until this moment just how feminine sipping a drink could be.

She swallowed and said, "He had the whole thing planned. He had a good disguise and another five people who looked exactly the same. Pepper spray is an untraceable weapon, and he escaped along the river where there were no surveillance cameras. Unbelievable."

"Do you think your dad could have pulled it off?"

She grimaced and then shook her head. "Anything's possible, but I don't think he was actually the one to commit the crime."

"Why not? He has a slim build and is around six feet tall. Just the way you described."

"Yeah, but this guy was fast. Athletic. I keep in shape, and he easily outran me. That tells me—"

"He's in shape, too." He shook away an image of her long legs wrapped around his waist. "Does that describe your—"

"Stop calling him my dad. He's Hank Scott."

"You mean he's a stranger to you?"

With the tip of her index finger, she drew circles in the condensation on the outside of her glass. "I wish." She took another sip and stared into the distance, seemingly lost in thought.

"Yesterday was tough," he said, bringing her back to the present.

"It's been a tough week." She turned to face the street, her shoulders slumping.

The blank look in her eyes made him feel somehow disheartened. "I'm sorry."

She shuddered and then smiled as though visibly shaking off her melancholy. "Don't be. It's just one of those things."

"Your whole life has been turned upside down," he said, stating the obvious.

"Yes, but maybe it's an opportunity. I never planned on becoming a cop, and I really didn't plan on returning to Magpie."

"You didn't?"

"No, I wanted to go into social work and specialize in addiction."

"How did you end up here?"

"When I was in my last year of university, I called Chief Hunt and told him everything I knew about Hank's operation. I figured the information would help."

"Everything?" He would have to call Sergeant Mia Olsen and make sure she questioned Ex-Chief Hunt. He pictured his commanding officer. Her petite frame and blond hair gave her the air of a genteel lady, which she was, in some ways. She was known for being fair, straightforward, and brilliantly incisive, but when crossed, she could verbally claw a man like a tiger. No one ever challenged her or doubted her authority.

Georgina took another sip of her drink and then said, "I don't know that any of it helped. I was twenty at the time. Grace and

I were taken away when I was seventeen. My information was probably out of date."

"You were put into care? Why?" He wondered if she'd admit to putting her father in the hospital.

"My mom had a breakdown. It had been coming on for a while. Hank had been gaslighting her for years, drugging her, lying to her, and wearing her down with snide remarks. There were a lot of days when she was too sick and disorientated to feed herself, let alone function. It was all so gradual, but at the same time relentless. Grace and I tried to help her, but we were kids and—"

"There's only so much you could do." His heart squeezed for the lost girl she'd been. As the oldest, she'd probably felt a responsibility to hold things together.

She shivered again, as if chasing away her childhood memories. "To be honest, Chief Evans' reaction to me after the robbery has put me on edge more than anything else."

"Why?" he asked the question even though he knew the answer. Chief Evans had been obvious in his disdain, which wasn't helpful to Liam's investigation.

"I realized how much he dislikes me."

He didn't argue with her assessment, but he wanted to hear her slant on the chief's behavior. "Do you think it has something to do with your father?"

She rubbed her temples. "Probably. Hank is vicious, mean, and totally without scruples. But no matter how the chief feels, I can't change who I am. Unless my mother had an affair, which I doubt, Hank is part of my DNA."

When they'd entered the coffee shop, she'd been strong and confident. But now with her hunched posture and the way she stared down at her hands, he sensed her defeat. She couldn't get away from her past. No one could. He rubbed his palms over the legs of his shorts, hoping the action would refocus his mind. He was allowing himself to get caught up in her drama instead of getting information. He needed to change the subject. One of the largest drug thefts from the evidence locker had taken place on Christmas Eve last year. If he could get her talking about her future plans, then he could steer the conversation to the time in question. "Where are you spending Christmas?"

She gave him a look that suggested he was crazy. "Christmas? That's six months away."

"I'm trying to look on the bright side. If you change jobs, you might not be on shift, and you could spend it with your sister."

"She has her boyfriend. I'll probably spend it alone. It's not a big deal. How about you?"

"If I'm on the same shift rotation, I'll be working," he lied. He had no idea where he'd be at Christmas.

"Will your family be disappointed?"

"My mom and my sister might, but my dad wouldn't care. My mom is also the worst chef in history. The last time she tried to cook a Christmas turkey she forgot to turn on the oven and then couldn't figure out why it was still raw after eight hours."

Georgina's eyes lit with humor. "Didn't she check on it?"

"Apparently not." He took a sip of his coffee. It was cold.

"I'm not much of a cook either. Although I've been known to do a cook-from-frozen turkey and a packet of stuffing."

"Sounds delicious." He imagined sharing Christmas dinner with her in her small home.

She smiled, her spirits seeming to lift. "Actually, it is. Do you miss them?"

"Who?"

"Your family?"

"They're very disappointed by my career choice so I don't miss being reminded of that. Dad can hardly look at me." There was something about her that made him divulge too much.

"But you're a cop."

"I know." He didn't elaborate. He was making a mess of this. They were talking about his background when they should be discussing hers.

"What did you do last year to celebrate Christmas Eve?" He almost groaned at his own clumsiness. He was acting like a rookie instead of a seasoned professional.

She smiled, not seeming to notice his awkward attempt to interrogate her. "Normally, I don't do much at all, but last year was different." She pulled her wallet from her backpack and opened the flap to a photograph. Two smiling women stood in front of a large swimming pool, which was surrounded by tropical plants. "This is me and my sister in Mexico. It was spur of the moment. Her boyfriend, Rob, paid for the trip, but then he had to back out at the last minute. You know Greg?"

Liam nodded as his heart thumped against his ribcage.

"Anyway, he and his wife were having some problems. She wanted him out of the house, so he covered for me. It was, hands down, the best time I've ever had."

He grabbed the wallet and stared at the smiling faces of Georgina and her sister in the photo. He tried to disguise his shock as his heart thudded hard against his ribcage. She looked exactly as he'd imagined. Her breasts were small and perfect. He ached to run his fingertips over her honey-toned skin. But more importantly, she hadn't been working on one of the dates when the drugs had been stolen from the evidence locker. She hadn't even been in the country. He'd have to corroborate the details, but if it were true, she'd just blown a hole in his investigation.

CHAPTER FOURTEEN

George snatched her backpack from under the table. "We should head out."

They'd finished their drinks, and the conversation had run dry. Liam seemed to be caught up in his own thoughts.

A young couple holding hands entered as she approached the door. Once again, she was reminded of her own sorry personal life. She hadn't been in a relationship for so long. Maybe it could happen with Liam? She glanced at his long, tanned legs and perfectly shaped behind, which was accentuated by a pair of khaki canvas shorts. He wore a green T-shirt, which revealed his toned biceps. He didn't have the body of a weight lifter, but of a man who exercised to stay in shape.

No, they couldn't get involved. Not only was the timing wrong, but it was obvious he didn't trust her. He'd pushed his way into her house last night as though she were a criminal, and she wasn't sure what to do about that. She had confronted him about it at the time, but the incident still rankled. He'd said it was a protective reaction. Whatever the hell that meant. Her gut was telling her that there was more to it than he admitted. If he was going to be a permanent fixture in her life, then she would have to deal with his actions and her response. But, as it stood, nothing in her world was permanent, and neither was sexy-as-sin Liam, so it didn't matter.

She needed to figure out what was next for her. She felt like she was floating down a stream without a rudder. Maybe she should learn to go with the flow and take it one day at a time.

Go with the flow.

She pictured the robbery. The landscaper rushing for the guard and the way he'd run for the river.

Liam grabbed her shoulders and stared into her eyes. His brow crinkled. "Did you hear me? Are you okay?"

She put a hand to her head. "Could it be that easy?"

He frowned. "Could what be—?"

"I know what he did." She grabbed his hand and dragged him to the edge of the sidewalk and then turned to face the river.

"Who's 'he'?" Liam stood next to her, still holding her hand.

"The guy." She stepped towards Liam's truck, forcing him to let go. "The landscaper-robber guy. He went with the flow."

He gave her a look that suggested she'd lost her mind. "What flow? Are you sure you're not—?"

She brushed away his concern with a wave of her hand. "I'm fine. Can you take me to the bank? I'll show you what I mean."

"It's a short walk."

She winced but didn't say anything.

His gaze softened. "You're still sore from yesterday, aren't you? No problem." He pressed a button on his key fob and unlocked the truck.

In less than a minute, they were in the bank parking lot.

"Pull up near the river." She pointed the way.

He did as she asked.

Once he'd shifted into park, she climbed out and looked across the waterway.

Liam joined her on the grass.

"Do you smell that?"

He shrugged. "All I can smell is BBQ."

"It's from the Park Valley Campground on the opposite side of the river from the bank. The owners rent out float tubes."

He gave her a sideways glance. "Float tubes?"

"You must've seen them. They're round with a hole in the middle, like inner tubes for a tire, but they're made to float on the water."

"Yeah, so what?"

"What if our guy got one and used it to float over to the campground on the other side of the river? What would he be dressed in? A pair of jeans and a T-shirt. He'd look just like everyone else."

"He'd be soaking wet and have the sack of money." He raised an eyebrow in question. "That would be difficult to hide."

"It would've been heavy, but that probably wouldn't matter if he had a car waiting for him. I mean, look at that boat launch." She pointed to a short dirt strip that had been cleared of trees and bushes. Campers could pull up to the shore and back their boat into the river. Vehicles were parked off to the side, within easy walking distance. There were also several float tubes tied to a small dock, which was on the right side of the landing.

He gave a low whistle. "That's a heck of a plan."

She smiled, pleased he was taking her idea seriously. "All he had to do was stuff the money in his car and go. There are no cameras to worry about and no description of his getaway vehicle."

"He had decoys dressed just like him. He had an escape route that avoided all the street cams in town, and he only had to use minimal force."

"Yes, it was well thought out and executed," she agreed. "Like a military operation."

He turned and scanned the area. "The question is, do we have any young, fast military types in the area?"

"I can only think of one. Randy Woychuk. He lives on a farm just west of town. I heard he was back, but I haven't seen him in ages. He was at least five years ahead of me in school."

Liam smiled. "My shift doesn't start until four. You're the navigator. I'll drive."

Chief Evans would have a fit if he knew what she was doing. She should take all her theories and information to the RCMP investigators who were in charge of the case, but playing detective with Liam was a welcome distraction.

CHAPTER FIFTEEN

Liam parked his truck next to the red painted barn, which stood out against the green fields and the tiny yellow buds on the unripe canola crop.

Georgina's tank top rose as she climbed out of his truck, revealing a well-toned, flat abdomen. He wondered if her skin was as soft and silky as he imagined.

"Hello," she called.

He hushed her as he jumped out of the pickup. He would've preferred for her to wait in the vehicle until he'd made sure they would get a warm welcome, but he doubted she would follow his orders.

He had to wonder why he was being so protective of her. When he'd seen Buddy leaving Georgina's place last night, he'd been overcome with jealousy. It was a new emotion for him. One he'd never felt before, but he accepted it for what it was. He was envious of Buddy's relationship with Georgina, which was something he needed to bury and deal with later.

She scowled at him and called out again, "Hello."

"In here," a male voice called from the barn.

They followed the sound, entering the cool interior. The building was actually a large garage with a cement floor. There was an assortment of farm machinery parked about the place. Liam recognised a harvester and a water truck, but the rest seemed to be an assortment of tools that were designed to be attached to a tractor. What they were used for, he couldn't say.

"Know anything about valves?" A man was bent inside an engine, the upper half of his body hidden by the hood.

"Hi, Randy, I don't know if you remember me. I'm George... Georgina Scott, and this is Liam Mackie. We're with the Magpie Police Service."

"Yeah, you're Hank's daughter. I've heard of you. But I can't say I remember you." Randy straightened, limped over to a work bench, and grabbed a rag.

He had a well-built upper body with broad shoulders and muscled arms. He would pack a powerful punch. Unless Randy was faking his limp, there was no way he could've outrun Georgina.

Her gaze connected with his, telling him she'd come to the same conclusion.

"What?" Randy must have noticed their exchange because he snapped, "Look, I'm not in the mood to put up with any do-gooders or any of that crap."

Georgina held up a hand to stop him. "No, it's nothing like that. I just feel foolish. Really."

"About what?" Randy threw his rag on the workbench and crossed his arms. Everything in his body language suggested he was pissed off and wasn't scared to show it.

"What happened to your leg?" Liam asked. He was being direct to the point of being rude, but he wanted to divert Randy's anger away from Georgina.

"Lost it in an accident in the Solomon Islands. File it under *shit happens*." There was a hardness to Randy's expression that telegraphed his resentment.

George gave a weak smile. "Sorry, I hadn't heard. We'll leave you in peace." She turned and headed for the door.

"I should thank you," Randy called after her.

She stopped and faced Randy, her eyebrows furrowing in silent question.

"Your dad approached me when I got back. Told me he could get me all the oxy I wanted for free." Randy hobbled toward her.

"Shit." Liam muttered the curse under his breath. This was going to turn nasty. He closed the gap between them. His instinct to shield her overwhelmed his intellect.

Georgina stared at Randy for a moment and then held her hands up in a motion of surrender. "I don't have anything to do with—"

"Then I remembered what my nephew told me about the drug

business. A dealer will give you drugs for free. They'll do anything to get you hooked so you can't walk away, and then they'll take everything you have, including your future."

Georgina stared at Randy, not responding to his words.

Randy stopped a foot away from her and took her hand in his. "You taught him that in school. It saved me. Thank you."

Liam relaxed his fingers. He'd been prepared to beat Randy, but that hadn't been necessary.

A jolt reverberated through his body as though he'd been hit by lightning. He'd been a blind fool. Georgina was not the thief. He knew it, not just instinctively, but logically. She had no access to the evidence locker, and she'd been out of the country when one of the thefts had occurred. More importantly, she worked for the greater good and made a difference to the community. She helped people like Randy understand the dangers and the business of street drugs. That knowledge had prevented him from making a mistake.

Georgina stared down at her hand, which was still in Randy's grasp. She sniffled. Liam realized the emotion of the moment was getting to her. She took a shuddering breath and gave Randy a watery smile. "You're welcome." She gave his hand a final squeeze and then walked out of the barn.

Liam waved goodbye to Randy and followed her.

She didn't speak until they were back in the truck and bouncing down the rutted, dirt driveway. "That was a waste of time. I feel bad for even thinking it might be him."

"Me, too," he said, steering his truck onto the paved road, resisting the urge to discuss Randy's revelation about Hank pushing oxy. The information probably wasn't new to her. She'd grown up with Hank and understood the evil behind his business. It was Liam who was playing catch-up.

She stared out the window, making him wonder if she was still teary after her encounter with Randy. "Besides, even without the limp, it couldn't have been him. Like I said, the guy I saw was slim at the shoulders."

"We could talk to Buddy." He regretted the suggestion as soon as the words were out of his mouth. There was no way he wanted to question Buddy while Georgina was with him. "Unless you can think of anyone else."

She swiveled in her seat to face him, her eyes narrowed, and she tilted her head to one side. "There *is* someone we should talk to."

Thank God. "Who's that?"

"John Rogers, Mattie's son. He was in town just before the robbery. I bumped into him at the coffee shop. I got a druggie vibe from him, but that's just an impression. I don't know for a fact that he's using."

"It's nearly lunchtime. Do you want a pub lunch?"

"Sounds good."

They drove on in silence.

He was glad he'd asked Georgina for coffee this morning. Not just because he enjoyed her company, but it had become blatantly obvious he should have done his own homework when it came to his investigation and not relied on Chief Evans' assessment.

The report he'd received from Evans hadn't mentioned her work in the community and her school outreach position. He'd also failed to do his due diligence when it came to her whereabouts for one of the robberies. She had swapped that shift with Constable Greg Nicholson. Liam would have to widen the scope of his investigation and look into it with an open mind.

From now on, everyone was a suspect.

CHAPTER SIXTEEN

"Do you want to sit inside or on the deck?" Liam asked. He held her hand as they walked into the Rockin Horse Saloon. The pub had set up some tables and chairs on the grass beside the parking lot.

Georgina squinted against the bright afternoon sun. "Inside. It's busy out here, and we'll need some privacy to talk to John."

Liam led the way through the darkened pub to a corner booth where he sat facing the door. He signaled the waitress, smiling at her. "We'd like to order."

"Hi, Carly." Georgina greeted the short, curvy young woman who'd had her nose stuck in a book when they entered. "How's the spring course at university going? Have you done your midterms?"

Carly placed two laminated menus in front of them. "Yes, but my finals are coming up fast."

"You have Philpot?" Georgina smiled at the young woman. "I can still see her glasses slipping down her nose."

"Yeah, she's so stern she scares me." Carly seemed to have no reservations about Georgina. Although, that was true of nearly every interaction he'd witnessed. Most of the townsfolk liked her.

"Try not to let her manner intimidate you. She looks scary, but she's fair. Her course on women and crime was a real eye-opener, and she was my most encouraging professor."

Liam was mesmerized by the conversation. It was hard to picture Georgina as a carefree student. No, she'd never been happy-go-lucky. Her childhood had been too harsh for that.

"Hey, is John around?" Georgina asked, her manner casual.

Carly shook her head. "No, I haven't seen him since yesterday morning. Mattie's here somewhere. I'll tell her you're asking for her." Carly fished her notebook from her apron. "What can I get you?"

"I'll have a burger, fries, and a Coke." Georgina handed her the menu.

"The same for me," Liam said.

Carly left to fill their order.

Liam's gaze roamed the pub. "I find it interesting that the waitress assumed you wanted to see Mattie. You never mentioned her."

Georgina shrugged. "I visit her every now and then."

"Is the Rockin Horse a problem spot? Do you get called here to a lot of fights?"

"On occasion. But Mattie employs bouncers on Friday and Saturday nights. I haven't seen the statistics, but I would say I have more chance of being sent to break up a fight in the campground than here." Once again, she was preparing him for the job.

His chest tightened at the reminder that he was lying to her about who he was. Maybe he'd been telling her the truth because deep down he wanted to be honest with her. "That makes sense. People tend to get all gooned up around the campfire."

Mattie Roger's strode toward their table. Her bearing reminded him of a big predatory cat. "What brings you here?"

"Lunch." Georgina smiled. "Have you met the latest member of the Magpie Police Service?"

He held out his hand. "Liam Mackie. We met the other night."

"Pleased to meet you, again." She gave him a firm shake. "You were with Greg. George and I go way back."

"So she told me." Liam remembered his last conversation with Mattie. There'd been no introductions. Maybe that was down to Greg, or perhaps it was because Mattie didn't care. He knew Georgina trusted the older woman, but there was something about her that made the hair on the back of Liam's neck prickle.

Georgina finished a sip of her cola and said, "Actually, I wanted to talk to John."

Mattie took a small step back, crossed her arms, and narrowed her eyes. "What about?"

Georgina shrugged, seeming carefree and relaxed. "Nothing important. I bumped into him, and he'd mentioned he'd moved back into town."

Mattie smiled weakly. "Oh, honey, if you're thinking of dating him—"

"No." Georgina's lip curled, revealing her obvious distaste. "Nothing like that. I've always thought of him as a brother."

Liam had a sneaking suspicion that Mattie was trying to embarrass Georgina in order to throw her off her game. Everything about her, from her posture to her attempt at distraction, seemed suspicious. There was no way he'd allow her to get away with that. "Actually, Georgina mentioned John was into…into…"

"Real estate," Georgina supplied as she graced him with a grateful smile. "And Liam's looking for a place to live so I thought this would be an opportunity for John to get a commission."

"He's not here. He's in Las Vegas." Mattie snapped out the words.

"He didn't mention that when I saw him yesterday." Georgina smiled again, ignoring Mattie's manner.

The older woman's eyes widened. "You saw him yesterday? When?"

"Just before the bank robbery. He was at the Jumping Bean. He looked a little…a bit off, as if he'd had a rough night."

Mattie thumped the table. "You have to give up this obsession you have with John. He would never look at anyone with a pedigree like yours."

Georgina flinched as if she'd been slapped.

Liam leaped out of the booth, placing himself between Mattie and Georgina. "We're leaving." He took a step forward, forcing Mattie to retreat. "She's a cop, a damn fine one, and she has no interest, whatsoever, in your idiot son. You owe her an apology."

He grabbed Georgina's hand, hauling her out of her seat, and headed for the door. Mattie Rogers had deliberately humiliated Georgina. It was a distraction, and one that made him wonder what she was hiding.

CHAPTER SEVENTEEN

Liam seemed to be distracted by his own thoughts on the drive to her house, which was a relief. Mattie's hostility had left George shaken. She understood the older woman's need to protect her son, but to belittle George's concern by claiming she was fixated romantically on John and then publicly insulting her "pedigree" was another blow. She'd always considered Mattie a friend, but perhaps she'd been wrong in that assumption. Feeding a hungry kid went a long way toward gaining that child's loyalty, but how far should that allegiance go?

If she was being honest with herself, the person who had surprised her the most was Liam. He had been outraged on her behalf. That was a new experience for her, and she didn't know if she should thank him or just keep quiet. Was his reaction that of a cop standing up for a fellow officer, or did it mean he cared? She wished she had more experience with men, then she might understand his motivation a little better.

Maybe she hoped there was more to his indignation because she wanted him to like her. She mentally rolled her eyes at her own stupidity. She was thinking like a teen girl with a crush. Just because he was attractive in a hockey-player-with-a-broken-nose kind of way didn't mean anything would happen between them.

Liam pulled into her gravel driveway, parking behind her beat-up Subaru.

"Thanks for everything," she murmured. The day had caught up with her. Her butt and lower back still ached from colliding with the car and then slamming onto the pavement yesterday. All she wanted to do was soak in a warm bath. Maybe she'd just grab an icepack instead and fall into bed. It was only two in the afternoon. Too early to sleep, but she really wanted this day to be over.

"Your eyes are changeable like the sea," Liam announced with no warning.

"I don't know what that means," she said, instantly defensive. Men did not notice her, not physically. She was tall without any curves and tough enough to beat the crap out of most of them. Apart from her long hair, there was nothing feminine about her, and yet a small part of her yearned to be seen as a woman, especially by him.

"Your eyes change color with the light. When you're in a dark room, they appear to be green, and when you're in sunlight, they seem silver or gray. It's captivating."

She stared at him for a long while, uncomfortable with his attention even though she craved it. She understood that he'd spoken the truth without any poetic whimsy. But his observation still made her self-conscious. No one had ever noticed her eyes. "You have to be really confident to use a line like that. Have you forgotten what I said about charm?"

He laughed and then said, "Technically, it's not a line if it's true. And I wasn't being charming. I was just stating a fact. I didn't say I liked it, and…" He sighed and then continued, "Sometimes, I'm just being nice. I get that you don't trust sweet talk, but where's the line? Your eyes really do change color depending on the light. It's been bothering me. I'm a cop. We're trained to give descriptions, like he was tall with dark hair and dark eyes. I can't do that with you."

She smiled. "Oh, so you're saying you can win this argument by using logic."

He gave an uninhibited belly laugh. Heat coursed through her body as every cell came alive. She was aware of his musky scent, the lines around his mouth, and a tiny drop of perspiration on his right temple.

She'd never been this attracted to any man before. He smiled, the dimple on his left cheek deepening. *Oh, man.* That wasn't fair. How could she resist someone so utterly compelling?

"This has also been bugging me." He reached over and brushed a stray hair away from her cheek. The movement brought him within inches of her face. Without thinking, she leaned in and kissed him on the mouth. It was just a peck, but lasted too long to be chaste. She should stop and pull away, but instead she grabbed his shirt and tugged him closer.

He jerked back and stared, his eyes wide with surprise.

Her skin burned. She gasped, covering her mouth. She wanted to turn away and bury her head in her hands, but she couldn't. She froze. That was the stupidest thing she'd ever done. What a fool she'd been. He wasn't attracted to her at all. She searched for the right words, needing to apologize. "I—I—"

His lips crushed hers as he drew her into his arms. His tongue parted her lips. Her nerve endings responded, springing to life. He'd moved fast and without warning. She was playing catch up. Her left arm was wedged against the seat. She struggled to free it, wanting to align her body with his. Their awkward position in the truck meant she was unable to get close enough to him. Deepening their embrace, she needed to feel his naked chest against hers while she explored his form. She cradled his face with her hand, enjoying the roughness of his stubble. His thumb circled her nipple through her shirt. It would be so easy to straddle him and tear his T-shirt over his head…

She wrenched herself away, jamming her back against the passenger door in her attempt to put some distance between them. The handle dug painfully against her spine. *Dear God*. She was thinking, *planning*, on having sex in a pickup, in her driveway, with a man she barely knew. Her life was a mess. She was a mess. "I have to go." She grabbed the handle and opened the door so fast she almost fell out of the truck. "Bye. Thanks for the coffee and for driving me around."

"See you." He waved and smiled, seeming confident, centered, and not at all affected by their kiss. *Bastard*.

She rushed up the porch steps, all the while fumbling in her backpack, trying to find her keys.

Finally, she located them and managed to open the lock. She gave him a final wave, slammed the door behind her, and threw her bag on the ground. *What was I thinking?*

CHAPTER EIGHTEEN

Liam listened as Andrew Mackenzie, otherwise known as Buddy, unlocked his front door and entered the dim hallway. Buddy lived in a newer apartment on the other side of the highway from downtown Magpie. It was a nice place, but it had no security, which had made it easy for Liam to pick the lock unseen. Breaking into people's houses was a skill he'd acquired while working undercover. It wasn't something he would normally use, but he didn't want to be seen waiting for Buddy outside his apartment.

He tried not to think about the searing-hot kiss he'd shared with Georgina this afternoon. After he'd left her place, he'd put in a call to his unit at the RCMP headquarters in Edmonton and talked to Sergeant Olsen. Mia was now looking into Georgina's whereabouts last Christmas. She was also checking out former Chief Hunt, Chief Evans, and everyone at the Magpie Police Service. Plus, everything they had learned or suspected about the armored car robbery was being forwarded to the detectives in charge of the case.

Liam sat on the couch. He'd been waiting for Buddy to return for the last twenty minutes. It was gone ten, but he could still see well enough in the dusky light. "Don't turn on the light."

"What the fuck, man? You scared the shit out of me." Buddy clasped his heart as he leaned against the entryway wall, catching his breath.

"You need to stay away from Georgina. She has enough on her plate without being mixed up in this mess."

"I just lent her a bike. It's what friends do." Buddy collapsed into a brown leather armchair opposite. "And for the record, I'm not dragging her into this. I dragged you and the fucking RCMP into this."

Liam had interviewed Buddy when he'd made his complaint

at the RCMP headquarters in Edmonton. Apparently, he was a whiz at anything engine related. Harry Bawa, his boss at Magpie Marine repair, had given him the space to set up the bike rental business as long as he didn't fall behind in his work as a mechanic. Buddy was well-liked and had a reputation for being honest. People trusted him. He was also enterprising and ambitious, but he wasn't a criminal.

"Not that you had much choice. Hank Scott started leaning on you, threatening you—"

"I know. I was there. If I don't help him, he'll kill me. You were supposed to catch him and stop him."

"As it stands, it's your word against his."

Buddy wrapped his arms around his knees. "What can I tell you? He barged in here a month ago and said he had a plan. He needed my bike rental business. I only operate it in the summer. And as you know, summer in Alberta is fucking short, which means whatever he's planning has to be soon. Is that why you're posing as a Magpie cop?"

Liam didn't answer the question but instead he asked one of his own. "What do you know about the robbery?"

Buddy shrugged his slim shoulders. "Same as everyone else. Why?"

"Georgina chased the guy. She said he was about six feet tall with a slim build. She said there was something familiar about him."

"Fuck you!" Buddy poked the air with his finger. "I came to you for help and you've done fuck-all. Now you're accusing me of stealing?"

Liam could see his point, but he wouldn't be doing his job if he didn't ask. Any criminal activity threatened the perception of Buddy as a reliable witness and put his case in jeopardy. "Answer the question."

"When did it happen?" Buddy spat the words, his disgust obvious.

"Yesterday, around ten in the morning."

"I had to take my mom to the doctors in Edmonton. Her appointment was at the same time. I can give you the name of the doctor."

Liam smiled. "Thanks. For the record, Georgina said there was no way it could be you."

He grunted and then said, "It's good to know I still have one friend."

"How long have you known her?"

"Since we were eight. Some kid was picking on me at school, and she beat the crap out of him."

Liam could almost hear Buddy grinding his teeth. "So you two go way back?"

He inhaled and then said, "The three of us, actually—George, Grace, and me. Why? Where are you going with this?" Buddy snapped, his suspicion apparent.

"Hank threatened you in order to get you to cooperate. Would he do the same to her?"

He laughed. "You're kidding, right?"

Liam gave a noncommittal shrug. He wanted Buddy to tell him about the incident between Georgina and Hank without any urging.

Buddy leaned back in his chair, relaxing. "When George was seventeen, Hank tried to sell Grace. I don't know who the buyer was, but George got wind of it. She pounded the crap out of Hank. You should've seen her fists flying. She unleashed all her anger and hurt, everything she'd been holding in. She lost control and beat him to a pulp. It happened in the pub parking lot. The cops just watched and didn't try to stop her." Buddy grinned at the memory.

"You witnessed it?"

Greg Nicholson had mentioned the incident, but that had been hearsay.

He nodded. "She told him if he ever went after the people she loved, she would kill him. She meant it, too."

"How badly was he hurt?"

He shrugged. "Spent a week in the hospital."

"I'm surprised she wasn't charged." He was even more surprised Hank Scott hadn't exacted some kind of revenge. For someone who was a major player in the local drug business, not punishing her could be seen as a weakness by his rivals.

"Are you serious? Everyone in town knew what was going on. He burned his daughters with cigarettes. He beat them. He spiked his wife's food and drink so she didn't know which way was up. We all knew what was happening, but no one did anything about it."

"What happened to them afterwards?"

"Chief Hunt whisked them away and hid them while Hank was in hospital, recovering. Word was he changed their identities and everything."

"But you kept in touch."

He shook his head. "No. I didn't see George again until she started working for the Magpie Police Service."

"Where did she go?"

"I'm not sure. You'll have to ask her."

What was Hank up to and why drag Buddy into it? He had a feeling this had more to do with revenge than it did business. Liam stood and headed for the door. "Watch your back. You've got my number. Call me if you get a sniff of trouble."

Once he was in his truck, he dialed Sergeant Olsen's personal number.

"What?" she answered on the first ring.

"I have more information."

"Cut the crap," she snapped. "What you really mean is you have more questions, and you need me to do some research for you."

He didn't comment on her correct assessment. He'd called her at home because he needed this information. He suspected that Hank Scott was setting Georgina up, but why now? Why wait years to get back at her?

"I have four kids. That means I never sleep, and I don't need you interrupting me when I do get the chance to close my eyes. No matter how good looking and charming you think you are."

"I've been told that charm is a veneer, a disguise people use to hide who they really are."

"Sounds about right. What do you want?"

He told her about the incident between Hank and Georgina and then said, "Can you look into Georgina and Grace Scott and see if they were in the foster system? Georgina would've been about seventeen. And check out the mother. What's her current situation?"

"Got it." She hung up without saying goodbye.

CHAPTER NINETEEN

Liam swiped his card on the side door keypad that gave him access to the police station. Everything was quiet, as expected, for Tuesday at midnight. All the civilian employees had gone home, and there was only a skeleton staff at the detachment. Most of the officers on duty were out on patrol.

He had focused his investigation on Georgina because Chief Evans had been so sure of her guilt. He'd trusted the chief's analysis. That had been a mistake, one he needed to correct…now.

He pictured Georgina's shocked expression after their kiss. He got the impression she wasn't someone who dated very often. And he couldn't see her letting just anyone into her life. She was tough to the point of being world-weary and prickly as hell. He'd probably be the same if he'd grown up with Hank Scott as a father.

He made his way through the lunchroom to the large open area, which was divided into cubicles. The scuffed beige walls and mismatched office furniture gave the place a shabby, lived-in feel.

Talking to Buddy had been enlightening. Her childhood had been a nightmare. That much was obvious, but she was a fighter. He was drawn to her, and not just because he wanted to get her sweet little butt into bed. Yeah, the sexual attraction was off the charts, for him at least, and after the kiss they'd shared, he believed she felt the same. The chemistry worked, but it was so much more than that. Not only had she overcome her upbringing, she had also returned to the place where she'd been tortured and was trying to save the citizens of Magpie from a drug dealer. She was a hero who deserved better than to be accused of a crime she didn't commit.

He suspected she was being set up, and the person most likely to do that was her father. Everything led back to Hank Scott. He was the one who benefited from the thefts, and if what Buddy had told him was true, Hank would probably like to see his daughter punished. What better way to do that than ruin her good reputation and everything she had worked to achieve?

But why now? Could it have something to do with the former chief of the Magpie Police Service, Aiden Hunt? The thefts had been going on for quite some time and had only been brought to light because of Lillian Field. He would have to get Olsen to send someone in to question both Lillian and Hunt. Something was off. He just didn't know what.

He sat at an empty desk, switched on the computer, and signed in. Every keystroke was recorded and could be traced. This was a preventative measure that stopped officers from abusing their power.

He accessed the list of thefts. The drugs had been placed in the locker when the arrests had been made. Evidence was not viewed and accounted for every day. It wouldn't be checked out again unless it was needed for an investigation or for trial, which meant they only had approximate dates and times when the drugs were taken.

Then he searched the database of the Canada Border Services Agency, looking for Georgina's holiday to Mexico a year ago. The dates pinged on the screen. She'd left the country four days before Christmas and returned the day after. The drugs were discovered missing on Christmas Eve. They had been placed in the locker the day after she'd left the country and were stolen before she returned. She couldn't have taken them. Had the perpetrator timed the thefts to implicate her? If so, why had they taken them when she was away? It had been a short, unplanned trip. She'd swapped with Greg Nicholson. Had the switch appeared on the duty roster? Maybe the real perpetrator was unaware of Georgina's vacation. That was a lot of *ifs* and *maybes*. He couldn't allow himself to get ahead of the facts.

Chief Evans had indicated he was grateful Lillian had noticed the missing drugs. It was a testament to her efficiency. Once evidence was catalogued, it was stored in secured lockers in a sealed room until it was needed for trial. Then it was sent to the court for processing. Only three people had access to the evidence: Lillian Field, the desk sergeant, and the police chief. If the suspect pled guilty, it might never be looked at again, which meant rich pickings for an unscrupulous officer. Wait...if Lillian had known the drugs were missing last Christmas, why did she wait to report them? Or maybe she had reported them to former Chief Hunt, and he'd ignored the situation or was implicated. More questions with no obvious answers.

He glanced around the deserted bullpen. There was only one officer, an older cop, Sergeant Jake Taylor. He was big, bald, and gruff, and permanently worked night shifts. The Magpie Police Service was small with less than twenty employees. He needed to go through each person and see if they were on shift when the drugs were taken. He tapped the keys. He was in for a long night.

CHAPTER TWENTY

Georgina opened her large living room windows, allowing the cool morning air to flow through her small house. The wind-driven waves on the lake could still be heard above the cacophony of loons, ducks, and blue jays. A squirrel sat in a large maple in her yard, chirping out a warning to the magpies and crows who'd gathered in a nearby spruce tree.

Under normal circumstances, this would be a wonderful way to wake up on a Wednesday morning. But no matter what the test results revealed, she wouldn't be able to drive for six months. Given Chief Evans' animosity toward her, she doubted he would place her in a desk job.

Living here had always been worth it because the location offered her the peace and tranquility she needed to unwind from her stressful job. But with no car, staying here just wasn't feasible because she didn't want to walk into town in the winter when the temperature dipped to minus forty. Luckily, her lease had expired, which meant she had defaulted to a month-by-month agreement. She would contact the couple who owned the property and give her notice.

Maybe she should move away, especially since she'd pounced on Liam like a starved animal. She turned away from the view, grabbed her phone, and accessed the music app. Pulling up her favorite rhythm and blues playlist, she pressed play, hoping the music would soothe her.

She'd focused all her energy on getting justice and ignored her other needs like love and companionship. Was it any wonder she'd lost control? This was the first time she'd received any attention from a man in years.

"Idiot." She yanked open the doors of her large hutch. She'd lovingly refinished the solid maple piece, staining the horizontal surfaces in dark cherry while coating the sides and door fronts in a clear varnish.

She'd gotten up early and baked cookies in case anyone visited, which was stupid of her. She had no friends, just colleagues, who were probably busy with their families. She could die here, and no one would find her for days, maybe weeks. She was like an old, lonely woman. All she needed was a herd of cats to complete the picture.

Seeing Hank behind bars had been a childish dream. Now it was time to grow up. When she was at university, working on her degree in sociology, she'd vowed to dedicate her life toward making the world a better place. Sitting holed up in this house feeling sorry for herself wasn't accomplishing anything. She should volunteer. There was always someone who needed a helping hand.

She marched to the kitchen with a new purpose. So what if she'd kissed a man because she was an isolated woman who hadn't had any male attention in years? The next time they crossed paths she would apologize for making unwanted advances and move on.

She grabbed some old, clean margarine tubs from a cupboard next to the fridge and tipped the cookies from the baking tray into the containers. One of them missed, hit the counter, and bounced. Three of them landed on the ground and skidded across the floor like hockey pucks. Baking really wasn't her thing. She didn't have the patience or desire to understand the process. The only reason she'd even tried was because it seemed like something normal people did, but she wasn't "normal." She was the daughter of a drug dealer. She'd learned how to fight by watching her father beat up his minions. He'd also taught her the basics of running a business where the return customer was everything.

She hadn't had an average upbringing. She couldn't cook and didn't care about fashion or makeup, but she could make a damn fine cup of coffee. When she was in the mood, she would use her French coffee press, but today was about speed and convenience. After extracting her bag of medium roast coffee beans from an air-tight jar on the counter, she set the grinder to just the right consistency, poured in the aromatic beans, and hit the on button. Then she slid the gold-plated filter into the basket. Once the coffee was ready, she placed it in the drip coffee maker to brew.

Then she set to work packing for her bike ride. She wore leggings and a tank top, which were comfy and practical. She added a lightweight, long-sleeved shirt to her pack along with a can of bug spray, sunscreen, and a water bottle.

The coffee was almost brewed. Searching through her cupboards, she found an old thermos. She would share her coffee and cookies with Smokey. If friends didn't come to her, she would go to them.

Her keys and wallet went into the front pouch of her bag. Then she headed out onto her porch to unlock her bike, grateful she had transportation. Chatting to Smokey would help her mind from spinning and stop her self-pitying spiral. After talking to Smokey, she would go into town. The local food bank, the library, and the thrift store all needed volunteers. The best thing she could do was keep busy.

****

Smokey sat on an old tree stump, feeding logs into his campfire. He frowned as he watched her lean her bike against a large birch tree on his property. "I'm burning off waste. Don't give me a hard time about fire bans."

It wasn't unusual for backyard fire pits and charcoal briquette barbecues to be banned during a dry summer, but as far as she knew, there were no restrictions at the moment.

"I'm not working, Smokey." She slumped onto a faded green plastic lawn chair by his side, trying not to stare at his beard, which was peppered with toast crumbs. At least, she hoped they were toast crumbs. "I made some coffee and I baked. Do you want them?" She placed the items on the ground at his feet.

He eyed her suspiciously. "You baked?"

She shrugged. "Just some sugar cookies. I know you sometimes feed the ducks. I figured they'd be good for that if nothing else. Are you refinishing anything?" She changed the subject to a neutral one, not wanting to discuss her domestic failures.

"No, I can't find any interesting pieces. They need to have good bones. Too much furniture is made of plasterboard these days. What am I supposed to do with something that crumbles?" He poured some coffee from the flask into his mug and then passed the rest to her.

She took a sip, enjoying the smooth, earthy tones. "Smokey, I want you to be careful. I won't be on patrol anymore—"

"I heard you banged your head." He stared into the fire, not meeting her gaze.

"Yeah," His succinct interpretation of her situation didn't begin to describe the turmoil in her life, but discussing it wouldn't help. "An armored truck was robbed yesterday, which means they'll probably be upping the number of police in the area. The other cops don't know you like I do, so try and lay low. Stop crawling through restaurant dumpsters."

The old man stared at her, his rheumy eyes alert. "Where?"

"What do you mean where? In downtown Magpie where you normally—"

"No, I mean, where was the hold up?"

"Just outside the Credit and Savings Bank."

"I knew he was up to no good." Smokey drank his coffee and then swiped his mouth with the back of his hand.

"Who?"

He added another log to the fire. "I don't know who he was, but he did look familiar."

Familiar. That was the word she'd used to describe the perpetrator. "Did you see who did it? I chased him, but I couldn't see his face."

"I didn't see him recently. This was a week ago on a Sunday, I think." Using the thumb of his right hand, he counted off his fingers as he mumbled to himself, then sat in silence and stared at the fire.

George put the fact that he had drifted off down to his age and his mental health issues, but after a few minutes of silence, her patience was at an end. If she didn't give him a nudge, he might never speak. "Start at the beginning. Where were you and what were you doing?"

Smokey flinched and then straightened. "I was going through the dumpster at the boat repair place. Sometimes there's the odd piece..." He pointed to his garage at the rear of the house. "I once found a coffee pot there. It still worked. I sold it for—"

"What did you see?" she said, forcing him to stay on topic.

He stared into the fire. "A man. He had a can..." His brow crinkled as he frowned, remembering the incident. "A spray can of some sort. He was sprinting from the front of the bank down to the river. He did it three times."

"Like he was practicing?"

Smokey finally turned to face her, his faded blue eyes alert. "I knew he was up to no good."

She sat up straight. "Can you describe him?"

Smokey stroked his beard. "He was tall, good-looking, with brown hair."

"Would you know him if you saw him?"

"Of course, I would. I have excellent vision." He seemed insulted by her question.

"You'll have to talk to the police."

The old man frowned. As honest and harmless as he was, he was no fan of the Magpie Police Service or the RCMP. "Why can't you tell them for me?"

"I didn't see him. I can't describe this man to a skilled technician who can recreate his likeness. Besides, the detectives in charge of the case might have a suspect. Your ability to ID him will make a difference."

"There was something about him, but I can't place it." Smokey shifted his position on his log so he was facing away from her.

She'd had the same feeling. "I think this crime was committed by a local. If that's the case, then we probably know him."

"I don't want any dealings with the cops." Smokey had experienced his share of officers who didn't understand that having a breakdown didn't make him a criminal, just ill.

"It's important you talk to them. I can't promise to be with you all the time, but I can go into the police station with you."

"I'll think about it." He stood and walked into his house, letting her know their conversation was well and truly over.

She picked up her backpack and slung it over her shoulder. *Change of plans.* The police station was near the highway. It wouldn't take her long to get there, not with Buddy's bike.

CHAPTER TWENTY-ONE

George wiped the sweat from her brow as she entered the police station. The temperature was climbing, as was the humidity. Thunderstorms were forecast for late afternoon, and she wanted to get home before they rolled in.

She approached Lillian who sat at the reception desk behind a glass wall.

"Hi, how are you?" There was no way George could avoid the inevitable small talk.

"Great, I'm surprised to see you here. I thought you were on leave." Lillian smiled, but it didn't reach her eyes.

"I am. I have some information for whoever's in charge of the armored truck robbery."

"I heard you chased the guy."

George wished she could put her finger on what it was that bothered her about the older woman. She was always nice and seemed interested in George's life. Her unease was instinctual rather than anything concrete. "I'm kinda in a hurry."

"Oh, right." Lillian scurried into the back. Although she couldn't see it from the lobby, George knew that behind the door was a wide-open space filled with an assortment of desks, office chairs, and computers. It was the communal area where she had written reports and filed paperwork.

Chief Evans slammed through the door with Lillian following close behind.

George's heart dropped when he waved her into the station with a scowl. He didn't acknowledge her in greeting, but everything in his demeanor, from protruding eyes to his flared nostrils, indicated he was royally pissed. She followed the chief past the bullpen to his office at the far end. He slammed the door behind her and pointed to a chair opposite his desk.

His face was flushed, and his jowls looked heavier, giving him the appearance of an angry bloodhound. He lowered himself into his fancy leather seat. "Lillian says you have information on the robbery?"

She sat, but he was too agitated for her to relax. "Yes, do you know Smokey, the old man who searches the dump?"

The chief shook his head.

How could he not know the residents of the town? George dismissed the question. He was the chief, but maybe he was more concerned with paperwork than policing. "He's a feature around here. He lives along the lake and searches through dumpsters. He looks rough, but he's harmless."

He studied her for a long minute. At last he said, "You think you're pretty clever, don't you?"

George didn't say anything. The hairs on the back of her neck stood on end, but she remained silent. Gripping the armrests, she pressed her back into her chair in a vain attempt to distance herself from the attack she knew was coming.

"You've been playing the victim, claiming to hate your old man, when all the time you've been stealing for him. And now you have a witness to a robbery. How convenient is that? Hank Scott is behind ninety-nine percent of the crime here, and his daughter is a cop! No wonder we've never had anything on him."

George leaped out of her seat and backed away from the rabid chief of police. She buried the hurt and pain caused by his words. Her primary focus was to escape. It was a reflex born out of experience. Every time her father was angry, he lashed out. She knew it was illogical, but she feared the chief would do the same. She flung the door open.

He followed her into the bullpen. "You'll never work here again."

She stared around at the startled faces of her fellow officers. She made eye contact with Liam. He was here, watching this awful scene play out. She was acting like a child who was scared of the boogeyman when, in fact, she was an adult who had rights.

"Enough." She held up a hand to silence the chief. "I've done nothing to justify your contempt."

"Oh, so stealing drugs from the evidence locker isn't a betrayal of all our hard work?"

The air whooshed out of her lungs. She stared at the chief, unable to respond.

"There's nothing I hate more than a crooked cop," he continued.

She shook her head. "I'm not— I never— What?" She took another step back. "Drugs are missing?" She heard the disbelief in her own voice. This had to be a nightmare. Narcotics had been stolen, and she was being accused of the crime. She opened her mouth to protest and then closed it again. She was being blamed because of her relationship to Hank. No other reason.

"Did you think we were too stupid to put it together, or do you just think you're smarter than everyone else?" He stepped closer, his face so red she thought he might explode.

She blinked at him. Her chest hurt and she felt dizzy. She wouldn't faint. Not in front of them. They...*he* would not defeat her. She inhaled deeply, hoping that would clear her head.

She turned away from the chief and cast her gaze over the room, taking in the faces of her colleagues, men and women with whom she had worked for years. Why would they think she was a thief? There was no evidence. There couldn't be because she hadn't done anything wrong.

She straightened, refusing to cower. "I haven't stolen anything."

"We'll see where the investigation leads," the chief snarled behind her.

"Investigation?" *Liam?* Once again, her gaze connected with his. She stared into his serious dark eyes and, in that instant, she knew. It was like a curtain being lifted to reveal his true identity and purpose. He wasn't a rookie cop. He knew, and saw, way too much. He was trained and able. She'd allowed herself to be distracted by his charm and his apparent attraction to her, when all the time he'd been investigating her.

She swallowed as bile rose in her throat, took a deep breath, squared her shoulders, and headed for the door. She stopped with one hand on the handle and turned to face the room. "For the record, I've always worked to put Hank Scott in prison, which is where he belongs. I haven't stolen anything, and if you really want to solve the armored truck heist, you will talk to Smokey. He witnessed the robber practicing his getaway without his disguise."

With a trembling hand, she turned the door handle and marched out, praying she wouldn't throw up, or faint, in front of them.

CHAPTER TWENTY-TWO

Liam caught up with Georgina at the bike rack just outside the police station. She was kneeling on the ground as she rammed a D-shaped lock into her backpack.

He grabbed her elbow, forcing her to stand and face him. "Let me explain—"

"I don't want to hear it." She yanked her arm out of his grasp as she blinked back the tears that had gathered at the corner of her eyes.

"I never meant for this to happen." He swallowed, trying to rid himself of the sour taste in his mouth. He'd hurt her. That knowledge twisted his gut.

She took a step back. "I told you I don't want to hear it."

"There was a crime. I was sent to investigate." If only she'd let him tell his side, then maybe he could get her to understand he'd never intended to cause her any pain.

She shook her head. "And now I'm hearing about it." She poked him in the chest, her nostrils flared, and her free hand fisted. "Was kissing me part of that investigation?"

He almost sighed with relief. He'd rather deal with her anger than her tears. "No, that was real."

Her eyes widened. She stared at him as if he was an idiot. "How can it possibly be real when everything you've told me is a lie?"

"No, I didn't lie to you." He held up his palm in a halt motion, as if it would stop her anger and logic. "I was supposed to. I had a backstory and everything, but I couldn't. I really am from Vancouver, my parents are rich, and they don't like that I'm a cop."

"Good for you. But you think I'm a criminal." She schooled her features, shutting down any visible signs of emotion.

He wanted to tell her about his investigation and explain how he believed she was innocent, but he couldn't do that without compromising his investigation. If he was going to clear her name, he had to make sure he had an airtight case. "Nothing is as cut and dried as it seems."

"You shouldn't have kissed me."

He didn't say anything. There was no justifying his actions. He hadn't been a cop in that moment. He'd been a man who'd given into an overwhelming desire to taste her and feel her skin against his. Even now, when he could see the hurt in her pale gray eyes, he wanted to do it again.

"What's your name?" Her features were still blank, but there was a cold, hard look in her eyes.

"Liam."

"Liam what? Tell me your real name." She bit out the words.

"I'm Corporal Liam Mason with the RCMP."

She hung her head as though she was thinking. Then she toppled forward. He stepped closer, instinctively moving to catch her. Her right leg hooked around his ankles, knocking his feet out from under him. He slammed to the ground, landing on his back. The force pushed the air from his lungs.

By the time he was on his feet and breathing again, Georgina was three hundred yards away, peddling her bike past the community center. He could have gotten in his car and chased after her, but what was the point? He'd hurt her, and the only way to fix it was to clear her name and then beg for forgiveness.

CHAPTER TWENTY-THREE

George stumbled through her front door, slamming it shut. Only then did she allow herself to fall apart. A sob erupted from her throat. Liam had lied to her. He'd pretended to be her friend, and all that time he was playing a part. Worse, he'd kissed her. Yes, she'd been foolish enough to instigate it, but he'd reciprocated. Her stomach heaved, recoiling at the thought.

She slumped to the ground, allowing her tears to fall unchecked. Talk about a week from hell. No, it'd only taken Liam five days to wreck her life. He'd slammed into her and given her a concussion. Then she'd had a seizure and couldn't drive. After that, she'd witnessed a bank robbery and been taken in by a good-looking, charming son of a bitch.

It was one thing to lose her job because she was unable to drive, but quite another to get fired because she was suspected of stealing.

Her stomach rolled, reacting to her anger and humiliation. She took off her shoe and threw it across the room, hoping the physical release would rid her of some of her hurt.

Once again, Chief Evans hadn't afforded her the courtesy of talking to her in private. He'd yelled his suspicions in the bullpen in front of everyone. Now, all her former colleagues thought she was a thief. For the last five years, she'd worked to prove her self-worth. It had all been for nothing. As far as her fellow police officers were concerned, she was a criminal, the daughter of a drug dealer, and that's all she would ever be.

She wanted to pace. She wanted to go for a run. To be so exhausted she'd fall asleep and wake to find it was all a cruel dream. But this was real. There was no way she could face leaving the house. The world outside her small home was a ruthless, vicious place.

She hugged her knees to her chest as more tears stung her

eyes. She hadn't cried in years. She blinked them back. No one was going to beat her. Not Chief Evans, not the people of Magpie, and certainly not a sexy undercover cop.

Someone hammered on her door. She ignored it. It was probably Liam, wanting to explain himself again.

The banging continued, becoming more intense.

"Leave me alone," she shouted, although she had no idea if her visitor heard her.

Whoever it was hammered again, this time with enough force to rattle the hinges.

George pushed to her feet and peeked through the window. Her father stared back at her.

She wiped the tears off her face. Then she grabbed the baseball bat she kept in case he decided to drop in. She hadn't needed it until now. Gripping the bat in her right hand, she flung the door wide and poked Hank in the chest with the cap end before he could open his mouth. He stumbled back. She repeated the maneuver, forcing him down the steps and off her porch. He was fit enough and agile enough not to fall. *Pity.*

A young man with shaved fair hair stood behind him. George had no idea who he was. She hadn't seen him on her rounds but assumed he was her father's enforcer, his muscle. As if reading her thoughts, the bodyguard drew his pistol and aimed it at her chest.

George laughed and then said, "There are worse things than getting shot."

Hank grinned. "Like stealing drugs from the evidence locker?" He didn't look like a crook with his trimmed hair, clean well-cut jeans, and expensive collared shirt.

A ball of hate curled in her chest, making her heart pound. "I knew it was you."

Hank sneered. "Prove it."

"What do you want?" She had no patience for his mind games.

"I found Grace."

She failed to suppress a gasp. Every inch of her body froze as ice water ran through her veins. Grace had legally changed her last name to Campbell, the same as their foster parents, in the hope that Hank wouldn't find her.

She pictured her sister. People described her as an angel with her blond hair, her bronze skin tone, and dazzling blue eyes. But it wasn't her looks that made people love her; it was her giving nature and gentle smile.

"If you touch her, I will kill you." She held up the bat.

"You lay a finger on me, and I'll make sure you do time."

"It'll be worth it to be rid of you. I put you in the hospital once, and I'll do it again."

Using his thumb, Hank pointed to the muscle behind him who still had his gun trained on George.

She laughed again, but this time it was false bravado. Grace was in danger. "It's interesting you need backup to talk to me. Are you so scared—"

"Before you say something you'll regret, think of your sister. You and I can fight, but it's always the innocent bystanders that get hurt."

She remembered that night long ago and how he'd tried to take her sister away. They'd been hiding in the storeroom at the Rockin Horse. He'd burst in, grabbed Grace, and dragged her out. George had been seventeen, but she thought Hank had said something about making Grace presentable. She couldn't remember his exact words. But the feelings of terror and fear for her sister were etched into her soul. Even now, after all these years, remembering that moment filled her with a sense of overwhelming panic.

"What do you want?" she roared and straightened her spine, reaching for some much-needed discipline. She didn't often think about the night she'd punched him because she wasn't proud of her loss of control.

"I want you to admit you stole the drugs."

She could only think of two reasons why he would want her to take the blame. The first was that it would leave his person in place at the police station to steal again. Secondly, he would get rid of her. "What will I get if I do?"

"I'll leave your sister alone. Your life for hers. The math is simple." He grinned. If she didn't know him, she would never have guessed the extent of his malevolence because he seemed so normal, just a charming, handsome, middle-aged man.

She nodded, pretending to agree to his terms. "I'll need time to get my affairs in order."

He strutted to the Chevy Suburban and climbed in. His enforcer slid his weapon into his holster and got behind the wheel. She watched as they reversed out of her driveway.

She'd played for time, but there was no way she could go along with his plan. He was a liar and couldn't be trusted to keep his word. Once George was locked up in prison, he would go after Grace.

Only when Hank was gone did she allow herself to react. "Bastard." She raised a shaky hand to her mouth as a cry escaped her lips. *Oh, God.* He'd found Grace. Her legs felt like jelly, but at the same time stiff and awkward as she made her way back inside. She bolted the door behind her. What could she do?

In the past, Chief Hunt had protected her. He'd always had her back. Now she saw that he had, literally, kept the big bad wolf from her door. She was alone. She had nowhere to turn.

Yes, she did.

Liam was a RCMP undercover cop, but given their history, albeit short, she refused to ask him for help. Everything with him was too emotional, and she'd rather leave him out of it. But the Mounties were conducting an inquiry into the missing evidence. She would wear a wire, be the bait, and do whatever she had to in order to see Hank in jail. All she had to do was contact Liam's superiors.

She fumbled through her backpack, trying to find her phone. She might not reach the right person on the first try, but sooner or later she would be put in touch with someone who knew about the case. Then she needed to pack up her stuff. From now on, she had a new goal, saving her sister. Nothing else mattered —not her seizure, not her work with the Magpie Police Service, and not the bank robbery.

Her sister was still in Hawaii for another week or so which gave George time to organize. She was about to become Grace's bodyguard.

CHAPTER TWENTY-FOUR

Liam sat in a booth at the Rockin Horse, nursing a beer. There was no way he could justify Chief Evans' outburst at the station this afternoon. It had been unprofessional in every way. He'd called Olsen and informed her of this development. Evans had broken several investigative and code of conduct rules. He had informed George that she was a suspect, and in doing so had broadcast the fact that there was a probe into the entire detachment. There was no point in Liam working undercover if everyone knew about the investigation.

"This sucks." Greg Nicholson fell into the seat opposite.

"Agreed." Alan Hammond joined Greg, forcing him to slide over and make room. "George and I never got along, but she didn't deserve that kind of treatment."

"Do you think she's stealing drugs for her dad?" Liam asked. He might as well be open with his questions. The time for tact had passed.

"I just don't see how she, or any of us, could. We don't have access to the evidence locker. We put the stuff in a sealed box, sign it in, and then either the office manager or Sergeant Taylor assigns it an individual locker in the evidence room, which is secured with a top-of-the-line security system." Alan picked up a beer mat, creasing the edges of the cardboard square.

"You don't think it's possible to cheat the system?" Liam pushed.

"Maybe. If I was investigating, I'd want to know if anyone lost a keycard to the lockup." Greg gave Liam a knowing look. "If there's an extra key floating around, then you'd have your answer."

"Oh, yeah, if there's a spare key out there, then it's anyone's guess, but if there are only the original three, that should narrow your search." Alan's piercing gaze connected with his.

Alan had said "your search" not "the search." The difference wasn't lost on Liam. He'd underestimated these officers. They weren't some under-achieving country bumpkins. These guys were sharp. Sharp enough to realize Liam wasn't a rookie cop. Even though they obviously knew he was undercover, he wasn't ready to come clean yet, and they hadn't broached the subject.

"How about that shitbag, George?" Chief Evans interrupted. Judging by the sway of his gait and the way his words slurred, he'd already drunk more than he should. "Isn't she just the gift that keeps on giving? Chasing down robbers." He pushed into the booth beside Liam. "Finding witnesses."

Mattie approached. "Can I get you another drink?"

"I'll buy a round for my men." Evans made a circling motion with his index finger to indicate the group seated at the table.

"Not for me." Greg shoved at Alan's shoulder, telling him without words to move. "I promised the wife I'd get home early."

"Me, too," Alan said.

Liam knew for a fact Alan didn't have a wife. He suspected they were as disgusted by Evans' behavior as he was.

"What a bunch of pussies," Evans said as he watched his subordinates leave. He held up his glass. "I'll have another. What about George telling us Smokey saw the robber? As if that hobo knows anything."

Liam couldn't hold back a gasp. Sounding off to other officers about Georgina in a public place was bad enough, but revealing the name of a witness to a member of the public was unacceptable. "You've had enough."

"You don't get to—"

"Yes, I do. You're leaving now." He turned to Mattie, who was still waiting to take their order. "Call him a cab. We'll wait outside."

She nodded and headed for the bar.

The chief turned to face him, baring his teeth, ready to fight.

Liam grabbed Evans' left wrist, being sure to exert enough pressure to cause pain. The older man paled and backed down, nodding his agreement. Liam released him as they shuffled out of the booth. All the fight had gone out of the chief. He had the stunned gaze of a man who knew he'd gone too far and had just realized there was no going back. He headed toward the door under his own steam.

Once outside, Liam grabbed the chief's elbow and dragged him to the park across the street where no one could overhear them. "To be clear, I do not report to you. You are not privy to my ongoing inquiry, but your behavior tonight will be going in my report. You can expect to hear from my superiors, the town council, and the Alberta Law Enforcement Review Board."

Evans tugged his arm out of Liam's grasp. "Take it easy. Anyone can have a slip up."

"A slip up? In less than twenty-four hours, you have publicly revealed details of two investigations. I don't know what's going on with you. I don't know if you're just sloppy and unprofessional or if you're being malicious. There will be consequences to your actions. I can guarantee that."

Liam turned and stomped back to his truck, not caring if the chief took the taxi or returned to the pub.

He pictured the despair in Georgina's eyes when she'd realized he was investigating her. He should never have kissed her, but he hadn't been able to stop himself. Now he had to man up and deal with the fallout. He dug his phone out of his pocket and dialed Olsen's number. He would tell her everything. Not just about Evans' behavior tonight, but also his involvement with Georgina. Let the higher-ups figure out the best course of action. Sometimes the best thing to do was own your mistakes. This case was as fucked up as they came, and there was no hiding from it.

CHAPTER TWENTY-FIVE

George stifled a yawn as she sat on a stool at the polished wood coffee bar of the Jumping Bean Café. Mrs. King frowned as she prepared George's vanilla latte. No surprise there. But George had a purpose, and she couldn't let Mrs. King's obvious disapproval stop her.

Before going to bed, she'd managed to get hold of Sergeant Olsen with the RCMP, who seemed to know about the investigation into the stolen drugs. George had informed her of Hank's threat. She also promised to press charges and testify against him.

Her anxiety over the chief's accusations, the missing drugs, Hank and her sister, had all combined to keep her awake. When she did fall asleep, around three in the morning, her dreams had been filled with visions of Grace, beaten and bloody.

She'd given up on getting any rest after waking at six and had set to work cleaning her house. It wasn't just occupational therapy. Soon she would have to move, and she needed her damage deposit back.

Mrs. King finished making her beverage and placed it in front of her.

"I have a wonderful chest with a hutch. It would make a great display case," George said in a rush before her courage failed her.

Mrs. King's eyes narrowed. "Why are you getting rid of your stuff?"

"I'm moving."

"Why?" Mrs. King snapped out the word as though she was giving an order.

George gave her a questioning look. "I don't owe you an explanation."

The older woman sighed, giving up her confrontational attitude. "No, you don't, but you've done so much good here. I'll be sorry to see you go."

George was taken aback. She hadn't expected anything positive from a woman who had shown her disapproval by frowning every time they met. "If you must know, my work as a police officer is done."

"I heard about your seizure. Is there no other work you can do here? You can't just give up."

George saw no reason not to tell Mrs. King everything that was going on. The more people who knew about Hank's threat, the less likely he was to act. Then if anything happened to her or Grace, he would be the first person the police interviewed. "It's not about giving up. It's not about me at all. Hank found my sister, and he's threatened to hurt her."

Mrs. King gasped.

"I have to protect her. I've always made sure I wasn't being followed when I visited her. I never wanted my work here to affect her life, but it has. I can't be a cop anymore, but I can keep him from getting his hands on her."

"Where is she now?"

There was no way George would reveal her sister's whereabouts, even if it was an innocent question. "She's on holiday abroad with her boyfriend. She gets back in a week and a half and doesn't know about any of this. I figured I'd let her have this time. Why ruin her vacation?"

"And protecting Grace is your only plan?"

George shrugged. "It has to be."

"I understand. Family is everything." Mrs. King patted her arm. "You can put your stuff in my storage locker until this blows over and you figure out what's next."

It was an unexpected gesture, which made George realize how much she'd misjudged the older woman. "Thank you. I hope you're not just saying that because I'm going to take you up on it."

She thought about Hank, her fragile mom, and her sister, Grace. Mrs. King was right. Family was everything. Even when all you wanted was to get away from the horror of your past, you couldn't because it was an integral part of you. She couldn't escape them, no more than she could strip away her own skin.

The bell dinged, and a couple walked in and wandered the store, looking at gifts.

"I can't afford to pay for the space," George said, wanting to make her position clear.

"No charge. I'll just keep your things until you come back." Mrs. King gave her a genuine smile, which was shocking because it was so unexpected.

"I don't know if I'm coming back."

"You will if you want to. You're the strongest person I've ever met. If you can't stop him, no one can." She tapped George's hand. "You're family." Mrs. King turned and greeted her new customers.

George watched as the older woman told the couple about her ongoing sale. All this time, she'd believed that Mrs. King didn't like her, but that wasn't true. George prided herself on being a good judge of people, but if she was wrong about Mrs. King, what else was she wrong about?

The door dinged again, and Liam strolled in. She took in his broad shoulders, slim waist, and tanned, outdoor complexion. It almost hurt to look at him, not because they'd shared one kiss and she wanted more, but because he had given her hope that things could be different, that she could be more than just a woman trying to stop her criminal father.

He crossed the room to stand in front of her, his mouth settling into a grim line. "I thought that was your bike."

"You realize Buddy has over twenty bikes that all look exactly the same. It could be anyone's." She refused to meet his gaze, not wanting him to see her pain.

He shrugged. "Yeah, it could be, but it isn't."

"What do you want?" She knew she sounded abrupt to the point of being rude, but didn't care.

"I'll give you a lift home."

That was it, no apology for lying, no mention of how she'd tripped him yesterday. Nothing. "No, I'm not going home."

"Where are you going?" He stood over her as if he could use his greater size to bend her to his will. *Fat chance.*

She poked him in the chest. "I don't have to tell you."

"Where are you going?" Mrs. King asked and then smiled shamelessly.

George sighed. They were ganging up on her. It wasn't much of a secret, and Liam could easily follow her. There was no way she could outrun him on her bike. "I'm going to see Smokey. I have to tell him I'm leaving."

Mrs. King finished making an order and carried the drinks to the couple's table. Then she came to stand next to George and jabbed Liam in the arm. "Did you hear that? She's leaving. Hank Scott has not been brought to justice. He's still out there, selling drugs, ruining the town, and destroying lives. She's been working her ass off with no help from you, and now she has to leave. Tell your bigwigs at the RCMP, thanks for nothing." She turned on her heel and marched into her office, slamming the door behind her.

"Does everyone know I'm RCMP?" Liam said, staring after her.

"Apparently." When had Mrs. King realized Liam's true identity, and why had it taken so long for George to see the truth?

Liam placed his palms on her shoulders, gently massaging them. "I need to talk to you."

"What, so you can lie to me some more? Oh, my mistake. It's not a lie when you're investigating me." She broke away from him and headed out of the coffee shop, not wanting to spend any more time in his company.

He caught up with her on the deck, grabbed her elbow, and spun her around, forcing her to face him. "I was sent here to discover who had stolen the drugs from the evidence locker. Chief Evans believed it was you, but I know you're innocent."

She stared at the ground. Could she believe him? "How do you know? And how come you're telling me this? Isn't sharing this kind of information against protocol?"

"I know what happened with Hank yesterday. Sergeant Olsen has given me permission to talk to you about the investigation.

Like it or not, this all centers around you. Now, get in the truck, and I'll tell you the rest."

This was work. He wasn't here to beg forgiveness because he cared about her. He had tracked her down to interview her. A knife-like pain shot through her chest. She'd made a fool of herself over him. He didn't want her and never had. She thought about lashing out and pushing him away. But she needed to be smart. Having more facts might stop her from being charged with a crime she didn't commit, which in turn would help her protect her sister. Finally, she relented and said, "Okay."

He lifted her bright blue bike into the bed of his truck while she climbed into the passenger seat. She inhaled and then exhaled, blowing away her worry and self-pity. It was a mental exercise she had repeated a lot in the last twelve hours. It helped ground her. She had to bury her feelings and deal with them later. *No wallowing.*

"Smokey lives along the shore, doesn't he?" Liam reversed out of the parking spot.

"Yes, just follow Lakeshore Drive." She pointed the way.

"Are you sure this is wise?"

"What, seeing Smokey?

"No, moving." He made a right turn at the end of Main Street.

"What have you heard?" Yesterday evening, RCMP Sergeant just-call-me-Mia Olsen had asked a momentous amount of questions. And finally ended the conversation by cryptically telling her that someone would be in touch.

"Hank's threatening your sister, which actually means he's threatening you. He wants you to admit to stealing the stuff from evidence. You shouldn't leave. You should stay and make a stand."

"Make a stand?" She gave him a look that, hopefully, suggested he'd lost his mind "This isn't some wild west gunfight. I have to protect Grace, and the only way I know how to do that is to be her bodyguard, which I can't do and pay my rent. I've promised to file a report and testify against him. You're the RCMP. This is your investigation. It's up to you to charge him."

He ignored her logical argument and asked, "Are you planning to live with Grace and follow her around?"

"Yes." The lake was like glass today, reflecting the blue sky and the trees along the shore. God, she'd miss this place.

"How does she feel about that?"

"I haven't told her."

He grinned. "I'll bet you a hundred bucks that she refuses your help."

"It's not a choice." She stared out of the window, not looking at him, focusing instead on a pair of loons bobbing for food out on the water.

"I think you should hold off on making any hasty decisions."

"Smokey refurbishes and sells furniture all the time," she said, ignoring him. "I'm going to ask him to sell my big hutch and dining room table. They're a matching set. But if I can't find a buyer, Mrs. King said she'll give me free storage."

"You need to listen to me," he growled.

"You said you'd tell me about the investigation," she snapped.

"Drugs have been stolen from the evidence locker. They've been traced to your fath—I mean Hank. In my opinion, Hank is trying to frame you for two reasons. He's trying to protect his source, and your community awareness talks have taken a bite out of his business."

"And Hank makes a huge profit if he gets his inventory for free," she added.

"The chief thought it was you because all the thefts happened when you were on shift."

Her hands fisted at the memory of being publicly humiliated by her superior. "I don't have access to the locker. Any evidence I've collected is handed over to the clerk or the desk sergeant. In the five years I've worked for the Magpie Police Service, I've never once set foot in that room." She relaxed back in her seat and rubbed her temples, thinking about who could have committed the crime. Finally, she straightened when the pieces of information fit together to form a larger picture. "If I was a betting woman, I'd put my money on it being Lillian Field."

"Lillian? It can't be her."

She sighed. Fatigue from her sleepless night was catching up with her.

Liam slanted his gaze toward her. "You're way off base. She's the one who reported the thefts. Why would she do that?"

"There's an audit coming up. Someone from the Alberta Law Enforcement Review Board will be going through the cases, checking to make sure all the evidence is properly tagged, labelled, and accounted for. The missing drugs would've been noticed. She was just getting ahead of it. You need to look into her finances."

"Shit." He gripped the wheel. "If you already suspected her, why didn't you say something?"

"Because I didn't know a crime had been committed. Although, I've been wondering about her finances for a while. She's a single woman who drives a big, expensive vehicle. I thought she might have a rich ex or rich parents." She smiled at him, letting him know, without words, the remark was directed at him. "There could've been a legitimate reason."

"Lillian Field." He thumped the steering wheel. "I never, for one minute, suspected her."

"I could be wrong, but I'm suggesting you check her out. Something doesn't add up."

"Is it just her vehicle that puts her on your radar?" He stared at the road, his brow crinkling.

"She's always being fake-nice to me."

He shook his head as though he was trying to decipher a foreign language. "Fake-nice? Is that a technical term?"

"Yes, it's in the police handbook." She grinned, feeling some of the tension from the last few days ease from her shoulders. "She brings me cookies, always peanut butter—"

"What's wrong with that?"

"It seems nice, but I've told her more than once the smell of peanut butter turns my stomach."

"And if she was a friend, she would have bothered to remember."

She shrugged. "Either that or she wants to make me feel sick. I also get a feeling when I'm around her. I don't know. I can't—"

"Is she charming?" he said, referring to their conversation from two days ago.

"She's not in your league when it comes to charm, but she tries to be." A knot twisted in her stomach. Why hadn't she seen through Liam's lies and his undercover persona?

He stared at her. "You said charm was a veneer, like a mask for people to hide who they really are."

"You should know," she murmured, knowing it was a cheap shot, but she couldn't resist.

"For the record, I was...*am* working undercover. It's like I said yesterday, I never lied to you. My parents are rich. They did give me this truck. My dad doesn't approve of me being a cop. He wanted me to be a lawyer. I really do have one sister. I have a whole identity set up in case you checked up on me, but I blew it because, for some reason, I can't lie to you. And the kiss was real, and I want to do it again." He yelled the last sentence.

She smiled. "Yeah, I got that from the way you're shouting." His words gave her a measure of satisfaction. "Are you saying you blew your cover?"

He groaned. "I told you my real story, which thankfully doesn't matter now because you've been eliminated as a suspect."

They pulled into Smokey's crumbling cement driveway. There was no fire burning in the yard. No sign that he was home.

"Maybe he's out." She climbed out of the truck and made her way to Smokey's front door. Everything was quiet, but she had an eerie feeling that something was wrong, although she couldn't put her finger on what. She sniffed the air.

Liam stood close behind her. "What is it?"

"I'm not sure. Smokey lights a fire every night. There should be the lingering smell of smoke..." She sniffed again. "Nothing." She knocked on the door. There was no answer.

"Where else could he be?"

"He's probably in town, searching the dumpsters for anything worth selling," she said, pushing away her sense of dread. She was letting the drama of the last few days get to her, that was all.

"Maybe." Liam scanned the yard and then peeked through a dirty front window.

"Let's check out his workshop. He might be there fixing a piece of junk to sell." Despite the warm day, her hands were ice-cold.

Liam led the way to the back of Smokey's shack. The doors to the outbuilding were open, but everything was quiet. She stepped into the garage-sized structure. A buzzing sound caught her attention. She followed the insect-like noise behind a large table that Smokey used as a work bench.

She saw a pair of feet lying soles-up on the ground. They had a gray, dusty appearance. At first, she thought she was looking at a dirt-covered statue or a gray piece of furniture. Her mind couldn't translate what she was seeing.

She stepped closer, rounding the edge of the table. The whole body came into view. She gasped. "No. Dear God, please no."

Smokey lay on his stomach, his face twisted to the side. Something had oozed out of his mouth.

Liam grabbed her arm, tugging her back. "Don't touch anything. Back out the way you came in."

"We have to check him—"

"No. He's gone. All we can do now is make sure we don't contaminate the scene."

CHAPTER TWENTY-SIX

Detectives from the RCMP K Division had arrived. The Royal Canadian Mounted Police was divided into fifteen divisions. Alberta was designated as K division.

They questioned George about her interactions with Smokey, why she was here, what she had seen, and her impressions of his mental state. She'd also told them that she believed Smokey had witnessed the armored car robber without his mask. He could've identified him and suggested they talk to John Roger's about the robbery. He might be innocent, but he should at least be interviewed.

The officers were now talking to Liam. She watched him interact with the other members of the force. There was a comradery there, which told her they knew and trusted him.

She sat in Liam's truck with her window down. Sweat gathered on her brow and the back of her neck. A drop of moisture dribbled down her spine, and yet she shivered. It was a sensation that had nothing to do with the temperature of her skin and everything to do with the loss of a friend. There was also a deep, gnawing feeling that she'd missed something important, some clue, and that failure had led to Smokey's death.

Although she hadn't examined his body, she suspected Smokey had been poisoned. But why would anyone do that?

Chief Evans arrived. Every now and then he glared at her but kept his distance. This was an RCMP crime scene, and she was a witness, which afforded her a level of protection.

Her feelings for Liam were as confused as her messed-up life. She swung between being furious he'd lied to her and being grateful he believed in her. Although, it was getting harder to hold onto her anger. She'd instigated the kiss, and if she were honest, she was mad at herself for not seeing he was undercover. Even Mrs. King had known he was RCMP.

The petite blond woman, the same uniformed officer who'd been at the armored car heist, opened the passenger door of the truck. "I'm Sergeant Olsen. We spoke on the phone about Hank Scott."

George nodded but said nothing.

"Do you think he could be responsible for Smokey's death?"

George shrugged. "I don't know. Anything's possible."

Sergeant Olsen kept her features schooled, giving nothing away. She fished a business card from her pocket. "You're free to go. If you think of anything else, let me know."

"I will." She slid out of the truck and wrestled her bike out of the back.

She would go and tell Mattie she was leaving town. Then she would go home and finish packing. She couldn't do anything about Smokey, but Grace still needed saving. That hadn't changed.

CHAPTER TWENTY-SEVEN

The Rockin Horse was like a walk-in freezer. The air conditioner was either broken or set on the highest level. George rubbed her arms as she entered the darkened interior. There were less than ten customers, which made sense given that it was the slow time in the afternoon between lunch and dinner.

The ride here had been hot with very little breeze coming off the lake. Not that the weather mattered. She was too exhausted and sad to care.

Mrs. King from the coffee shop sat at the bar, sipping a glass of wine. She smiled and held up her drink. "Normally, I only indulge on a Friday, but it's been a tough week, so I'm starting a day early. Would you like to join me?"

"Thanks, maybe another time." George didn't smile back. She couldn't, not with everything that had happened. "Have you seen Mattie?"

"She's getting some stock from the back. She'll be out in a minute. I really wish you'd reconsider your decision to leave. You've been a blessing to the community."

While she appreciated Mrs. King's support, the change was so sudden and startling, it made George uneasy. Life was much simpler when she knew what to expect from people. "Why do you always frown—"

"Hey, George, what can I get you?" Mattie appeared carrying a cardboard box.

George curled her finger at Mattie, signaling for the older woman to follow as she inched to the far end of the bar. This conversation called for tact and privacy. "I told the police everything I suspect about John's addiction and his role in the armored car robbery. And I need to tell you that we found Smokey dead this afternoon."

Mattie grabbed a mug from under the bar and filled it with a dark, tar-like brew. Then she set it in front of George. "Coffee?"

"Thanks." George took a sip and winced at the bitter, stale taste.

Mattie sighed. "I suppose you had to tell them, didn't you? What tipped you off?"

"You did." George met her old friend's gaze.

Mattie stared at her hands, not maintaining eye contact. "Me?"

"It was the way you tried to embarrass me by claiming I was interested in John when you know I've always thought of him as a brother." She took another sip of her drink. "I also saw him in town just before the robbery. There was something familiar about the way the assailant ran. I finally put it together. I'd seen John when he was on the football team in high school. The police will need to know his whereabouts. I wanted to warn you myself. I owe you that much."

George took a long sip of coffee, wishing it was water. She was thirsty after her bike ride and hadn't had anything to drink for hours, not since this morning.

Mattie shrugged, seemingly nonchalant about her only son going to jail. "You gotta do what you gotta do. But there's no way my John murdered Smokey. He's been in Las Vegas since the day of the robbery. They can check that."

George hadn't said Smokey had been murdered. She'd just indicated he was found dead. So why would Mattie assume that? He was an old man. Wouldn't it be normal to think he'd died of natural causes? George pushed the thought aside, concentrating on her conversation with Mattie. "John committed the robbery and then flew to Vegas? Or did he drive?"

Mattie nodded. "He drove."

George controlled her features, not wanting to react to Mattie's admission. "Makes sense. It would've been hard for him to get the cash through the scanners at the airport. When did you know it was him?"

"Only after the fact. I'm his mother. No one can blame me for not turning him in." Mattie seemed lost and bewildered, a far cry from the strong, fierce woman George knew.

George's gut cramped violently. She thought she might throw up. "You're right. No one would blame you for that."

"Does your stomach hurt?" Mattie's lip curled in a sneer.

George stepped away from the bar, suddenly alert. Why *had* Mattie assumed Smokey had been killed? The older woman's mothering instinct had protected George and Grace when they were kids. How far would she go for John? "It was you, wasn't it?"

Mattie stepped out from behind the bar and whispered in George's ear. "You should've kept your nose out of it."

In that moment, George knew she'd miscalculated. She'd believed she was talking to an old friend, but that wasn't the case. She'd confronted a murderer who would do anything to protect her son. "You killed Smokey."

A stabbing pain sliced through George's skull. She groaned and grabbed her head.

Mrs. King rushed to her side. "Georgina, what's wrong?"

Mattie elbowed Mrs. King out of the way. "She's had too much to drink. I'll let her sleep it off in the back."

Another cramp twisted George's gut, bringing her to her knees. Her vision blurred.

"Someone, call the police," Mrs. King shouted.

"She's just drunk. I'll put her in a cab." Mattie grabbed George's arm and tried to drag her towards the storeroom behind the bar.

"You're lying. That girl has never had a drink in her life." Mrs. King chest-bumped Mattie, forcing her to release her grip on George's elbow. The two women were screaming at each other with Mrs. King trying to protect her. She might have laughed at the ludicrous scene if she didn't feel as though she was burning up and freezing at the same time.

Standing was impossible because her limbs refused to cooperate. She crawled toward the door, desperate to get away. Everything spun and slid sideways, making her stomach heave again. She needed help. Her phone. She could call Liam. He believed her. He would come to her aide. Where was her backpack?

"Someone call an ambulance!" She thought Mrs. King had

shrieked that demand but couldn't be sure.

The door to the darkened bar opened, flooding the pub with sunlight. George squinted as the silhouette of a man blocked the exit. He crouched down beside her. Even in her fragile state she recognized his broad shoulders, short-cropped hair, and dark eyes. *Liam.* Her vision blurred again as she gave up the fight and trusted him to help her.

CHAPTER TWENTY-EIGHT

Liam held onto Georgina's hand, watching the rise and fall of her chest. This was the third time in a week he'd visited her in the hospital, and he hoped it would be the last.

It was three in the morning, after twelve hours of treatment, the ventilator tubes had been removed and she was now breathing on her own. An intravenous line was still inserted into a vein in her arm, but the doctors were confident she would make a full recovery. It seemed that Mattie Rogers had added nightshade to her coffee.

"Have you arrested her?" Georgina's voice was thready.

"Don't worry about that." Liam gripped her fingers. The vise that had tightened around his chest loosened, allowing him to breathe. He pressed the button to raise the head of her bed and passed her a glass of water.

"Mattie killed Smokey," she said weakly.

"And she tried to kill you." He wasn't surprised she'd put it all together. What were the chances of having two poisoners strike in the same town on the same day? "We think Mattie took a meal to him that was laced with juiced potato leaves. After her arrest, her home was searched. We found the remnants in her juicer."

"Potato leaves?" She squeezed her eyes shut and then opened them again.

"I know, right?" He raised an eyebrow. "Apparently, you can only eat the tuber of the potato plant. The rest is poisonous."

She blinked away some of her grogginess, took another sip of water, and then said, "She was trying to protect her son, John."

"You always suspected him, didn't you?"

"Yes, there was just something so familiar about the landscape robber. John was a track and football star in high school. Mattie acted odd when we questioned her about John. I should have put it together before, but I was in denial. I didn't want it to be her." She pushed up on her elbow, winced, and then eased back down. A sign that it would take her a while to recover completely. "John did the robbery. He planned and rehearsed it. The way any team player would. But..." She frowned.

"Smokey saw him," he supplied.

"I can't say for sure, but I'm guessing Smokey didn't know John was Mattie's son. He arrived in town after John moved away. What I can't figure out is how Mattie knew about Smokey. I never told her."

"You can thank Chief Evans for that. After he lost his temper with you and announced my investigation to all the members of the Magpie Police Service, he went to the Rockin Horse, drank too much, and blabbed about everything you had told him. Plus, he named Smokey as a witness." Liam buried his anger over the breach of protocol. Georgina didn't need to deal with his rage.

"Shit. That means Chief Evans is responsible for—"

"Smokey's death. Yes. There's an inquiry into his misconduct." And he had been removed from his position, but Liam wasn't going to discuss the matter further. Not at the moment.

"Does that mean he's gone?" Her eyes were half-closed and her body relaxed, signs that she was getting tired.

He kissed her forehead. "I have to go...for now. I have an investigation to wrap up."

She smiled and curled on her side, getting as comfortable as she could with an IV in her arm. "Good luck."

He brushed a strand of long, dark hair away from her face. "I don't need luck because a very smart woman pointed me in the right direction."

CHAPTER TWENTY-NINE

It was close to midnight when Liam knocked on Chief Evans' office door.

With the chief gone, Sergeant Olsen had taken over. Evans' only saving grace was that he'd called in the RCMP when he'd discovered the thefts. His behavior after that was questionable at best.

Olsen sat at the Chief's desk, staring at a tablet.

Liam pulled up a chair beside her. "Any news?"

"I just got a call from the surveillance detail. She's left her house."

Under Liam's orders, Greg and Alan had signed in a large amount of meth while Lillian was working. Then he had spread a rumor that Georgina was out of the hospital, had quit her job, and would be returning her uniform tonight while the chief was at home. He had backed up the story with paperwork. In doing so, he had created a last chance for Lillian to steal the drugs. Technicians had set up cameras inside the evidence locker so they could watch the culprit take the bait. He just hoped the score was tempting enough for her to act.

After about ten minutes, the door to the evidence locker opened.

He held his breath as Lillian walked into the room and made a beeline for the meth.

"Go," Sergeant Olsen commanded.

Liam reached for his handcuffs as he ran out of the chief's office. He had her.

****

The interrogation took place at RCMP headquarters in Edmonton. The façade of Lillian Field, the plump, friendly woman who baked cookies for her co-workers, had fallen away. She glared at him, her hostility evident.

"Did you plan to set up Magpie Police Officer Georgina Scott?"

She shrugged. Her mouth was downturned, revealing her sour demeanor.

"You made sure she was on shift every time you stole evidence."

She remained silent, but he saw the defiance and hatred in her gaze. However, her pale complexion and trembling hands revealed something else—fear.

He could use that. "I'm going to see to it you're put in general population, and I will make sure everyone knows you were a cop."

"But I'm not a cop. I'm—"

"Denying it won't stop the beatings."

"You wouldn't." Her breathing hitched, and he thought she might hyperventilate.

He'd gotten to her. Time to turn up the pressure. "Tell us why you stole the drugs."

"He'll kill me."

"It's okay. I know who it is, and when I arrest him, I'm going to tell him you rolled on him." The threat seemed harsh, but he needed an airtight case, and without Lillian's testimony, all the evidence against Hank Scott was circumstantial.

"But I didn't. I haven't said a thing against Hank." Lillian pushed back in her chair, trying to distance herself from him.

"If you help us, I'll make sure you serve your time in a segregated wing." Liam grinned. Did she realize she'd just implicated Hank Scott? She was in a no-win situation. Now that he'd made her aware of it, he would give her a way out. "Tell me what I want to know, and I'll make sure you're safe."

Her shoulders slumped. "Hank Scott. I gave the drugs to Hank in return for a cut of the profit."

"And Georgina?"

"He wanted her destroyed. She'd publicly humiliated him twice."

"Twice?"

"First when she beat him up and then when she came back as

a cop. She was damaging his business."

"How?" A chill ran down his spine. He would have to make sure someone was guarding Georgina's house. Her father really hated her. Hopefully, he wouldn't be in a hurry to exact his revenge.

"Her talks to the kids in high school. Giving them details of his operation were taking a slice of his profits. That's why he started doctoring his marijuana. He needed to up his game."

"You'll have to give a written statement and testify against him."

She nodded as her chin lowered to her chest. Her whole body slumped.

Liam pushed away from the table. This was another nail in Hank Scott's coffin, but the investigation wasn't over yet.

CHAPTER THIRTY

After two days in the hospital, George had been sent home with orders to only eat bland, easy to digest foods, nothing spicy. She'd never cared about her diet so following that recommendation would be easy. Unfortunately, she wasn't allowed to drink coffee for two more days. She had no idea how she'd manage that.

Alan Hammond had given her a ride. He would never be her favorite person. He was too abrasive and didn't know the meaning of the word *tact*, but he was honest, and for that, she was grateful. He had checked out her trailer and made sure everything was safe before he left.

She sat in her living room, too exhausted to do much except gaze through the trees at the lake. It was so peaceful, watching the ducks swim in the reeds. A pair of magpies swooped over her yard and landed in a spruce tree. They really were pretty birds. According to her mom's old superstition, seeing two magpies meant joy, but there wasn't much of that going around.

The doorbell rang, startling her out of her spell. She eased off the couch and slowly made her way to the door. Peeking through the window, she was surprised to see Mrs. King's smiling face.

"Please call me Olivia." The older woman kicked off her sparkly, high-heeled sandals as she slipped into the house. Two plastic grocery bags dangled from the fingers of both hands. "I'll put the food in the fridge."

"Mrs. King...Olivia, let me repay you." George fumbled in her backpack for her wallet.

"Absolutely not. This is a gift, and you will accept it graciously." Olivia's voice held all the authority of a judge sentencing a convicted felon. George didn't have the energy to argue.

"I misjudged you," George said baldly as she followed Olivia into the kitchen. "But in my defense, you always seemed to be frowning at me. I didn't imagine that, did I?"

The older woman plopped the grocery bags on the kitchen floor, straightened, and sighed. "No, dear, you didn't. That wasn't about you. It was me. Whenever I saw you, I was reminded of my own cowardice. I knew you and your sister were in trouble as kids, but I didn't do anything. I should've at least called the authorities."

"If you'd done that, Hank would've turned on you."

"That's why I didn't. But I ought to have fed you. I never should've allowed you to end up at Mattie's door. That bitch was always in league with your father. Why do you think there's no cannabis store in town?"

"Are you saying they've been working together all this time?" George collapsed onto a kitchen chair. She wasn't sure what she was more surprised about, the fact that Mrs. King had used the word "bitch," or the revelation that Mattie had worked with Hank.

"It's nothing I can prove," Olivia continued as she placed a carton of eggs on the top shelf. "But look at that naked guy you chased last week. Where did he buy his drugs?"

George pictured Naked Nick on the bridge near the campground. His girlfriend, Veronica, had said he'd had a few beers. Had he purchased his beer and drugs at the Rockin Horse?

"Every time we vote on getting a legal government-controlled cannabis store, she whips up neighborhood opposition." Mrs. King placed a small jug of milk in the fridge.

"You support having a cannabis store in Magpie?" George asked. She'd always considered Olivia to be a straitlaced, buttoned-down woman. She was obviously wrong.

"I gave up drugs when I hooked up with John, but if it will put a dent in Hank Scott's business, then I'm all for it." Mrs. King slammed the fridge door with more force than was needed.

George gave her a watery smile. "In the end, you did step in. You were courageous. You saved me, and now you've fed me. Thank you."

Olivia sniffed while she folded and refolded a dishtowel, the emotion of the moment getting to her. After a moment, she gave George a watery smile. "Tell me about this hunky RCMP officer."

George pictured Liam with his long legs, broad shoulders, perfectly shaped butt and, most importantly, his lopsided smile. "There's nothing to tell except he's been undercover, so I don't really know him."

Olivia sat at the table opposite George. "How much do you need to know? He's one of the good guys, and he can't take his eyes off you—"

"He had to watch me for the investigation." He'd told her he wanted to kiss her again, but could she really trust him?

"Bullshit. He wants you. I know sexual attraction when I see it. Before I met John, I was a groupie travelling with a rock band."

"What?" George gasped. How had she been so wrong in her assessment of Olivia King?

Olivia waved away her obvious surprise. "I had a wonderful time. Sex is one of the great joys in life. Don't deny yourself because you're scared. Go for it."

George sighed, wishing she could be as carefree as her new friend. "I'm worried about getting attached. You know the old saying, 'If you can't stand the heat, stay out of the kitchen.'"

"If he leaves and doesn't come back, it's a non-issue. You'll just move on."

But her heart would be broken. That was the real reason she didn't want to get involved. What would she do if she fell for him? But it was too late; she already had.

"How did you meet John?" George asked, not wanting to discuss her feelings for Liam.

Olivia's gaze softened. "He was doing the band's accounts. He was so cute with his short hair, suit, and glasses. I seduced him the first day we met." Olivia grinned, showing no sign that she was embarrassed by the admission. In fact, the opposite was true. The way her toes tapped while she beamed from ear to ear suggested the memory delighted her.

"Was it all about sex?" She always wondered how people compartmentalized their emotions.

"I suppose it was at first. I think that's the way it is for a lot of people. But the more time I spent with John, the more I liked him. He was smart and made the band members seem like shallow jerks."

"Do you regret your time with the band?"

"No, not at all." She shook her head, her perfectly styled gray hair falling into place. "It was an education. The things I learned with them have kept our sex life alive. Plus, now that I'm older, I'm glad I lived it up while I was young." She grabbed George's hand. "Your life's been hard. You need to start making some good memories."

****

Greg Nicholson knocked on her door an hour after Mrs. King's departure. He seemed relaxed in a pair of jeans and a cotton shirt. "I thought I'd drop in on my way to work. I see Alan's on guard duty."

"Is he?" George had no idea what Greg was talking about. "Alan dropped me off ages ago, but I had no idea…" A thought occurred to her. "Am I under surveillance?"

Greg glanced down the driveway. He walked to the window and arched his neck, presumably trying to get a glimpse of their colleague. "You can't see him from here. It's protection duty until we have Hank in custody. Word is he threatened you."

George shrugged. Hank's threats were just same old, same old, and not something she wanted to discuss.

Greg must've sensed her reluctance because he smiled and held up a cookie tin. "Amy made these for you."

"Can I get you a coffee?" She wanted to ask about Liam but couldn't. All the questions that came to mind made her sound like a teenage girl with a crush.

"Sure." Greg smiled. "I'd never turn down a cup of your java."

"You can take one out to Alan, too." George made her way to the kitchen and filled the percolator with water and added some beans to the grinder. "I would have offered him a coffee sooner if I'd known he was there."

138

Greg opened the container, grabbed one of his wife's snicker-doodles, and took a bite. He waited until the appliance had stopped and said, "Did you hear?"

"Hear what?" She tried to ignore the fact that he was spreading crumbs all over her floor and focused instead on adding the grounds to her filter.

"Lillian was arrested. Liam set up a sting and caught her red-handed." Greg grabbed another cookie.

"Yes, Alan told me. That's a relief." There was no enthusiasm in her voice.

"Did he tell you that Evans quit?"

"Liam mentioned something when I was in the hospital, but I haven't seen him since." She flicked the switch, turning on the coffee maker, trying to ignore the pain of knowing he was still around but was ignoring her.

"Apparently, Evans is taking early retirement. I think he was forced out myself..."

George stopped listening. Being right about Lillian gave her no satisfaction, even though it meant she was no longer a suspect. Neither did the news of Chief Evans' retirement. Nothing seemed to matter.

At first, she'd wondered if she was feeling so lethargic and listless because of the poisoning or because Mattie, who she'd considered a friend, had tried to kill her.

But her mood had nothing to do with Mattie, Lillian, Chief Evans, or not being able to drive, but everything to do with Liam. She hadn't seen him since his initial visit to the hospital two days ago. There'd been no contact. No calls, emails, texts, or voicemails.

Nothing, nada, zilch.

Perhaps she was expecting too much. After all, they weren't in a relationship. She'd been a suspect, nothing more. He'd gotten to her in a way no one had and made her realize she was making a mess of her life by not sharing it with someone special. But her feelings, her attraction to him, had been one-sided. She had no reason to believe they were reciprocated. She'd been taken in by a sweet-talking undercover cop who knew how to say all the right things.

CHAPTER THIRTY-ONE

The pounding at her front door woke her. With her baseball bat in hand, she peered through the small window. Liam peered back at her. She flung it open and poked him in the shoulder with the bat. "What are you doing here?"

He blocked it with his forearm. "We need to go. There's not much time."

"I'm not going anywhere with you. It's one in the morning and I'm done with the roller-coaster ride. One minute I think you like me, and then you disappear. I've been home from the hospital for two days. What was that about?"

"I was ordered not to contact you until everything was in place." He wore his jeans and a T-shirt that stretched across his shoulders. She clasped her hands together to stop herself from reaching out and caressing his muscles.

"Ordered not to..." This didn't sound good. "Am I still a suspect?"

"No, nothing like that." He stood with his hands on his hips and looked up at the ceiling as though he was praying for patience. Finally, he said, "I told my boss about our kiss. She ordered me not to contact you. But I've been given—"

"You told your boss! Why would you do that?" Her cheeks warmed.

"I'm a straight arrow. I don't play games. The kiss mattered. You matter. That makes me compromised where this investigation is concerned. I'm not going to pretend it doesn't. What's happening is important to you and your family, so I obeyed orders."

The air whooshed out of her lungs. She was important to him. He had stayed away because he cared.

Their eyes met. She was struck by the strength of will and determination in his gaze. There was something else there too, heat. Before she knew what was happening, he had wrapped his arm around her waist and pulled her into his embrace. His mouth crushed hers, hot and hungry. His lips were cool and soft but the heat from his tongue ignited her senses, sending her into overdrive. In some ways she didn't understand what was happening between them, but she understood this. It was a physical need, pure and simple. Desire scorched through her. A wildfire of passion that awakened every cell in her body.

So she responded, giving into the impulse to pull up his shirt and slide her hands over his muscled torso. He yanked her top over her head. His thumb strummed her nipple as his tongue explored her mouth.

She sighed and then arched, giving him better access. Her logical thoughts dissolved as she lost herself in her need to touch and be touched by him. She tore at his shirt, tugging it up, and then running her fingers over his firm muscles.

He broke the kiss, resting his forehead against hers. "We have to go. We're going to be late."

She panted, but why she was out of breath she couldn't say. "Late for what? What's going on?" She thought of asking why he'd undressed her if they had to leave but discarded the question. Mutual attraction was...mutual. She shouldered half of the blame.

He tucked his T-shirt into his pants, "I can't say. You are permitted to observe from a distance. Trust me, you want to see this."

He'd said "can't," indicating he wasn't allowed to tell her, and there was something about the term "observe from a distance" that made her understand he was talking about police business.

"I'm not dressed." She was still wearing a pair of soft shorts but was naked from the waist up. She yanked her shirt over her head.

He gave her the once over and said, "You look fine. We have to go."

There was a tenseness to his demeanor that suggested something important was going down. "Okay. I just need a sweater and my keys."

Her breasts were small, but her nipples were so hard they could cut glass. There was no way she was going anywhere without making sure they were covered.

He nodded and watched while she gathered her stuff.

"How are you feeling?" He held her hand as they walked to the truck.

She laughed and then said, "You should've asked that before you pounced on me."

He gave her a lopsided grin as he opened the passenger door, grabbed her around the waist, and lifted her onto the seat.

"Does this have anything to do with Lillian's arrest?" she asked, curiosity getting the better of her.

"I want it to be a surprise." He cupped her cheek and brushed his lips against hers.

Without thinking, she hugged him and tugged him closer, wrapping her legs around his hips, aligning their bodies. His erection rubbed against the apex of her thighs.

His phone pinged. He groaned and then pulled away. "We will finish this, but you don't want to miss the surprise."

He slid into the driver's seat and punched a number into his phone, presumably calling the person who'd texted him. "I have her. We'll be there in five."

They drove to the Magpie Boat Repair and Sales, Buddy's place of work, in silence. Liam backed into a space next to a midsize boat. He placed his smartphone on the console between them, pressed a button to put it on speaker, and redialed the last number called. "We're in position."

"Just in time," Sergeant Olsen replied and then hung up.

This was obviously some type of raid. George couldn't see anyone in the parking lot or the office. Whoever Liam's colleagues were, they were good at hiding.

"Please don't arrest Buddy." She didn't want to see her friend caught up in a sting.

He swiveled in his seat to face her. The harsh lights of the parking lot illuminated his face, making his square jaw and broken nose more obvious. "You seem to think that you have to save everyone. But you're blind to the fact that you have friends in this town who've been trying to save you."

"I don't understand."

"Two months ago, Hank approached Buddy and threatened to kill him unless he allowed Hank to use his bikes."

Georgina gasped. "But you said Buddy was working with Hank."

Liam flinched. "I was jealous. I shouldn't be, and it was a stupid, knee-jerk reaction. I thought there was more to the two of you."

She laughed and then said, "You were jealous? That's awesome."

"Awesome? I was immature and childish, and you think it's 'awesome.' What's wrong with you?"

She rolled her eyes. "Isn't that the billion-dollar question? Between having Hank as a father, a mother who had a nervous breakdown, and falling for an undercover cop who was investigating me, I suspect there's a lot wrong with me. But it still bothered me that you pushed into my home that night like you thought I was a criminal. Compared to that, I'm fine with jealousy."

He grinned. "You fell for me. Good to know."

"Are you going to tell me what we're doing here?" she said, changing the subject.

"Right." He straightened in his seat. "Buddy didn't come to you when Hank threatened him. He didn't want you to have to deal with it. He reported it to us, the RCMP. He's been helping us set up a trap. We know Hank's suppliers, his customers, and his middlemen. Oh, and Lillian is going to testify against him."

He paused, scanning the area, and then continued. "Hank is coming here tonight because Buddy forced the issue. We had Buddy call him and demand a cut in exchange for using the bikes, otherwise he would go to the police. Someone like Hank understands greed."

"But what's to stop him from killing Buddy? I mean, this all started because Hank threatened him." Her heart rate increased as panic rose in her chest.

"We'll stop him. We have Hank under surveillance. He should be arriving anytime. Duck. I don't want to take the chance of Hank seeing you and taking off."

She did as he suggested and slid down in the seat. "No matter what happens, I want to thank you."

"For what?"

"For believing in me and allowing me to be here. That's not in your job description."

He smiled. "Any time."

Headlights illuminated the lot. George dipped lower, not wanting to ruin the operation. The side door to the repair shop creaked open. The minutes ticked by. George clasped her hands together, praying her old school friend would be okay. Shouts echoed through the night, but she couldn't make out what they were saying. A shot rang out. George jerked on the door handle. "No."

Liam clamped an arm around her and pinned her to the seat.

"Tell me Buddy isn't dead." She could hear the anguish in her own voice as bile burned her throat. She had so few friends. The thought of losing one as kind-hearted as Buddy made her feel sick.

Liam kissed her head in an attempt to calm her. "He'll be okay. I notice you don't care so much about Hank, do you?"

She didn't fight the hold he had on her. Logically, she knew Buddy was in the hands of professionals. All she could do was wait. "No, I don't care about Hank."

Maybe there was something lacking in her as a person, but she couldn't bring herself to feel any concern for the man who was her biological father.

Liam's phone buzzed. Once again, he answered it on speaker.

"We got him," Olsen announced.

Flood lights flicked on, illuminating the lot. RCMP cruisers raced in and parked in front of the entrance.

George sat up in her seat in time to see Hank in handcuffs

being led out of the building. A policeman slammed him against a car as they searched him.

Buddy walked out accompanied by two officers. He smiled and waved at her.

She waved back, grinning.

Buddy was alive. Hank was going to jail. Grace was safe. They had him. It was over.

CHAPTER THIRTY-TWO

Liam steered his pickup into Georgina's driveway. She'd been quiet on the ride home. He imagined she was overwhelmed with emotion, not just by the events of the night, but also everything that had happened in the last week.

She smiled as he parked the truck. "Do you want to come in for a coffee? I have decaf."

"Sure." There was no way he would say no to spending more time with her. He had to leave around six and go back to RCMP headquarters in Edmonton. After completing his paperwork and interviews with his superiors, he would be reassigned. Another investigation, another place. One more second with her was all he could hope for.

He tried not to squeeze her hand as they walked to her door.

She stopped before she put the key in the lock. "Thanks for including me in tonight's operation. That was thoughtful of you."

He cupped her face and then brushed her cheek with his thumb. "It was my pleasure."

She reached up and ran her hand over his stubbled jaw. He groaned as his penis sprang to life. Dear God, he wanted her, but he wasn't going to pounce on her like some rabid animal. She needed space to deal with everything that had happened.

She unlocked the door but didn't turn on the living room light. A faint glow from her bedroom light down the hall illuminated the house enough for him to see her looking up at him. Her changeable eyes seemed dark now. He could spend a lifetime watching them adjust to the light.

She reached up and placed a hand on his neck, just inside his shirt collar. He clenched his fists, resisting the temptation to tug off her shorts and impale her on his dick. Instead, he bent his head and kissed her, sliding his tongue between her teeth and wrapping it around hers. She groaned into his mouth.

He fought his own desire in an effort to be gentle as he slipped her sweatshirt over her head and traced small kisses down her neck until he reached the hollow at the base. He gave it a lick and was delighted when she shivered.

Her cool hands slid under his shirt to caress his back and roam his body until she circled his nipple and skimmed over it with the tip of her finger.

He pinned her against the front door and rubbed his chest against her breasts, wanting to excite her.

She was still wearing a thin shirt. He had yet to feel her skin. He stepped back out of her reach and stared at her, surprised to find he was gasping for breath. "I need to ask you something."

"What?" Her eyes narrowed as she assessed him.

"Am I taking advantage of you? It's just you've been through a lot this week, and I don't want you to regret...me."

She gave a short, harsh laugh and then said, "It feels like I've been fighting all my life. I haven't done anything else. I need to start making some good memories. I know you have to leave. I'm okay with that, but if I let you go without knowing what it feels like to kiss you, touch you, then I'll be sorry." She gazed at the floor and then faced him, twisting her hands together. "Hearing that aloud makes it sound like I'm using you. I'm not. I've just never been so attracted—"

He silenced her with a kiss, tugging her shirt over her head. She attacked the zipper of his jeans. He stepped out of them and wrapped his arms around her. Her breasts rubbing against his chest would've sent him into overdrive a few moments ago, but he was now a man on a mission. He wanted her to be able to look back on this moment as the best time of her life.

He walked her backward until her knees hit the couch. He grabbed the waistband of her shorts and slowly pulled them down, being sure to graze her inner thighs. Her head fell back as she moaned. Starting at her navel, he traced licks and nibbles up her body until he reached her breasts. He sucked her nipple into his mouth. She arched, allowing him more access. He increased his rhythm as he strummed her other nipple.

She writhed in his arms.

He picked her up. "Wrap your legs around me."

She did as she was told. He turned them around and sat so he was on the bottom. His hard-as-a-fucking-rock penis rubbed against her folds. She arched again. He was going to come soon.

"I want you on top." He knew women had a better chance of having an orgasm in that position. It was something to do with angles, but he couldn't remember what, and he didn't care.

She raised up on her knees and lowered herself, slowly, taking him inch by inch. She was so goddamn tight he thought he might explode.

She gave a little cry and stopped. He grabbed her waist and lifted her, hoping to ease some of her discomfort. Then he lowered her again. She repeated the process, raising and lowering herself, each time taking a little more of him until she was impaled on him.

"Are you a virgin?" He ground out the words between clenched teeth. She was just so fucking tight.

She rose and fell again and again, setting a steady rhythm. "No, but it's been years since..." A sob erupted in her throat. "I don't know how long I can last. I have to..." She increased the pace.

"Fuck." The feel of her warm, moist flesh wrapped around him was too much.

He grabbed her around the waist and set a frantic rhythm.

Within seconds, her orgasm rippled through her, milking him.

He joined her, his control breaking.

****

George opened her eyes a crack just in time to get a glimpse of Liam's perfect naked butt as he crept out of the room. Damn, he was a fine looking man.

The grey light of dawn leeched through the windows, telling her it was before five.

The shower turned on in the bathroom. Liam was leaving.

She'd known this would happen, but she'd hoped they could have breakfast together before he left. She sighed and rolled over, spreading out, taking all the room on her queen-size bed. She refused to be weepy. Should she thank him? No, that would be weird. A woman shouldn't thank a man for sex. It was great sex, the best sex she'd ever had in her life, but she had standards.

She rubbed her hands over her face in an attempt to get her thinking straight. The shower stopped. She heard him moving around the house. Finally, he tiptoed along the short hall to her bedroom.

The bed dipped when he sat on the edge. He bent and kissed her head. "Hey babe, wake up."

"I'm awake," she murmured, surprised at how sleepy she sounded.

He tucked the sheet around her and scooped her out of bed. "I made breakfast on the front deck."

She tucked her head into his shoulder and allowed herself to be carried. In a few hours he would be gone. She'd enjoy the pampering while she could.

He stood her on her feet the moment they were over the threshold. "I used all your emergency candles. I hope you don't mind."

This was like something out of a fairy tale or a movie. Lit candles were spread out over the deck. He'd even lined them along the railing. He'd created seating for them by strategically positioning her couch cushions along the floor so she could sit with a pillow behind her back.

"You must've searched all my cupboards to find the candles." She wasn't the type of woman who spent money on ornamental candles.

"Yep. And I made breakfast." He pointed to two plates. One piled with eggs, the other with toast. "Scrambled eggs and toast. That's all the food you have."

She blinked back a tear. This was, without a doubt, the best moment of her life. "This is...wow."

"Come on. It's getting cold."

He scooped her up again, carried her over to their makeshift seating and somehow managed to sit with her between his legs.

Her sheet had slipped exposing her breasts, but she didn't care. No one could see her from the road.

"What's next for you?" she asked and instantly regretted it.

He passed her some food and a fork. "I have to go to RCMP K division headquarters. There's a lot of paperwork, and we need to wrap up the investigation. Hank was part of a big network that stretches across Western Canada. There are a lot of threads that need to be tied."

She put her dish on the ground and knelt, facing him. "That's for later. Right now, you're with me. She unzipped his pants and was grateful to find his penis, erect, waiting for her. She straddled him. "We need to make one last memory before you go."

Using his fingertip, he brushed her hair away from her face. "This isn't our last memory. I'm coming back."

CHAPTER THIRTY-THREE

George's phone rang as she rode along the trail into town. She stopped in the shade of a maple, dug the device out of her backpack, and answered it. "Hi, Sis, how was Hawaii?"

"It was good." Grace didn't sound convincing.

"Hank's been arrested."

"Oh, my God. What was the charge? Will he be out on bail?" Grace's voice rose in surprise.

"No, it's been denied. How about you come over for a coffee, and I'll tell you everything I know."

"You usually come here."

Grace lived in Edmonton, a two-hour drive away, which normally wasn't a problem. George grimaced. "Shit. I forgot to tell you. A lot has happened since you've been gone. I lost my license. I'm not allowed to drive."

"You lost your license," Grace screamed. "Why didn't you lead with that?"

George held the phone away from her ear, counting to three to allow her sister to calm down. It was interesting that Grace thought her inability to drive was more important than Hank's arrest. "Maybe I should have but, as I said, a lot has happened."

"I have some business stuff to do today. I'll be over tomorrow."

"Great, meet me at the Jumping Bean."

"Isn't that Mrs. King's place?"

"Yes, it is. See you around ten." George hung up before her sister could ask more questions. There was a lot to tell, and she didn't want to do it over the phone. Plus, she had an electroencephalogram, known as an EEG, and a CT Scan booked for next week. Olivia had offered to drive her into Edmonton for the tests but she was hoping Grace could do it. Asking Olivia to drive her two hours into Edmonton and then wait around for her and drive her back, would take all day and seemed like a lot to expect of her new friend.

She climbed back on her bike and started peddling. Since Liam's departure three days ago, she'd made a habit of riding into town every morning and having coffee with Olivia.

Her phone rang again. She stopped under the shade of a maple to answer it.

"Hi." With just that one word, she recognized Liam's deep, smooth voice.

"Hi back." Heat flooded her body at the memory of their night together.

"Listen, I won't be in touch for a while."

"Are you going undercover?"

"Yes, but this is the last time. Once this is over, I'm coming back to Magpie and we can pick up where we left off."

She was silent, absorbing the small amount of information he had shared. If he was going undercover again, that meant he would be in danger. If anything happened to him, she would never know. She wasn't his next of kin. She was just a woman he'd met on a case.

"That is if you want me back," he said, sounding unsure.

"Yes, yes. I do. I just want you to stay safe."

"I will."

She could hear the smile in his voice. "Until next time, then."

He rang off.

She stood for a moment watching two magpies swoop overhead. *Two for joy.* Things were looking up. Liam was coming back and she'd have coffee with Olivia today and she'd see Grace tomorrow.

Surprisingly, she was reluctant to tell Grace about Liam. She wasn't embarrassed or anything like that; he was just too special to share. Which was a ridiculous thought. Almost everything that had happened between them had occurred in public. But his arrival had marked a time of upheaval in her life. He had changed her world. Before him, she had been a grey cardboard cutout going through the motions, fighting against Hank. No matter what happened in the future, she knew her life would never be the same again.

EPILOGUE

Georgina woke at two in the morning at the sound of someone hammering at her door. She raced through her house, flicked on the entryway light, and grabbed her baseball bat.

"Georgina it's me." Liam pressed his face against the small ornamental window.

She dropped her makeshift weapon, flung the door open, and jumped into his arms.

He held her tight for a long while, not saying anything.

Finally, she pulled away to stare up at him. Dark circles shadowed his eyes. His hair had grown, and instead of being shaved, it was now a short, dark pelt. He also sported a scruffy beard. Everything about him from his appearance to the blank stare in his eyes told her he was exhausted.

She cupped his face, giving into the need to touch him, comfort him. "What do you need? What can I get you?"

"Can I hold you while I sleep? I know it's been two months and I haven't been in touch but—"

She put a finger to his lips, silencing him. Then she took his hand and led him to her bed.

He could tell her everything in the morning. Right now, he needed rest.

IF YOU ENJOYED ONE FOR SORROW

You can read other books in
The Magpie Romantic Suspense Mysteries
Two For Joy
&
<u>Three For a Girl</u>
You might Also enjoy Marlow's
Gathering Storm Series

SIGN UP FOR MARLOW'S NEWSLETTER AND RECEIVE THE GATHERING STORM

starter library.
You can unsubscribe at any time.
https://www.subscribepage.com/marlowkelly

Made in United States
North Haven, CT
10 April 2022

18090458R00095